I0533594

DUST IN OUR VEINS

Tom Glass

Copyright © 2017 Tom Glass
All rights reserved.

Original artwork by Pariwat Mungkhun (Sakon Nakhon, Thailand)
ISBN: 0998846503
ISBN 13: 9780998846507
Library of Congress Control Number: 2017906966
Nok Kaew Publishing, LLC, Reston, VA

For Noke and Nat

"Back then, houses were all made of wood,
and they were built up off the ground on tall posts."

CONTENTS

INTRODUCTION: THUMPS

Lots of things in our village made thumps.

Frogs made thumps. At night they hopped into our bathroom, out behind our house, looking for the cool dampness in there. In the morning when they tried to hop out, they kept jumping against the walls or the back of the door. That's what made the thumps.

My sister and I heard them as we lay inside our mosquito nets. Sometimes whole groups of frogs were jumping, and it sounded like drumming. That was at dawn, and their teamwork woke us up gently. But if only one frog was jumping against the door, those thumps sounded lonely, and one of us got up to let the frog out. The day began right after that.

Mangoes made thumps, too. We had two trees off to the side of our house that took turns bearing fruit, one tree in even years and the other in odd. The mangoes grew ripe in the summer, and we picked most of them with a long bamboo pole that had a net on the end for the fruit to fall into.

But every year a storm came through and blew down some of the mangoes. It didn't matter which tree was ripe that year; the storm always came. The mangoes thumped when they landed.

"Let's go round them up," our father said as soon as the winds and the rain had died down. The mangoes were bruised where they had hit the ground, but he taught us to pick them up quickly, before the bruise had a chance to spread through the rest of the mango. He said that hitting the ground shifted the goodness around inside the mangoes so that the parts that weren't bruised became even sweeter and juicier than normal. We gathered them up and shared them with neighbors, who shared theirs with us, too. That night, there were storm-mango parties all over our village.

One other thing that made thumps was the big drum at the temple. The novice monks, boys not much older than I was, pounded the drum to let everyone know it was time to go there. We lived at the far end of the village, so by the time the sound of the drum reached our house, it seemed muffled, like the sound of those frogs when they jumped in the bathroom.

Pounding the drum was a glamorous job. I envied the novice monks when they came in last to the service, sometimes still sweating, after the villagers had all filed in. We took food to all the monks as a way to make merit and then sat listening as they chanted. We waited until they ate their fill before we could start in ourselves. No matter how hard we tried, we could never eat more than the novice monks who had drummed.

One year my sister and I tried to take storm mangoes to offer to the novices. Maybe our idea was to let them eat that extra-sweet fruit—or maybe we wanted to trick them into eating the bruises. But our father stopped us. With the long bamboo pole he brought down some unbruised fruit, and we offered that instead. On that same day, our mother explained that we should always offer the monks our very best food. From then on, we scanned the trees for top-quality mangoes and offered them proudly to the monks, sure we were making the purest kind of merit.

Our village, with all of its thumping, was called Slippery Stream Banks Village, part of the Slippery Stream District. Farther away than I could imagine was Three Streams City, the center of Three Streams Province.

When people hear that name, Three Streams, they naturally think, "Ah. Streams. Lots of water." But those are streams we have, not rivers, and besides, we have only three. Our province is in the middle of northeastern Thailand, an area called "Isan," the hottest and driest part of the country.

Everyone in Slippery Stream Banks Village, and for that matter all over Thailand, has some sort of nickname. My father and his two brothers, for example, have the nicknames Nueng, Song, and Saam, meaning *one*, *two*, and *three*.

My parents gave me the nickname Het, which means *mushroom*. And when my younger sister was born, they nicknamed her Tua-Ngok, meaning *bean sprout*. Armed with our parents and nicknames, surrounded by uncles and thumping, we were ready for life by the Slippery Stream.

FIRST THINGS FIRST

"First things first," our teacher told us when we started school. She taught us to stand at attention every time she came into the classroom. "And second things second," she went on. She taught us the words "at ease."

She took us through the first rough steps of education. "Next things next," was her philosophy. We learned how to sweep out the classroom and where to put the leaves we cleared from the school grounds.

She stopped us when we shouted or broke out in a chase. She said we were students now, not kids killing time at the edge of a ricefield. "Those things then," she taught us; "these things now."

We had already learned how to put on our uniforms of tan shorts and white shirts for the boys, blue skirts and white blouses for the girls. Many of us didn't have shoes; our feet had toughened and turned white from running barefoot down the dusty village lane. The boys had been given identical crew cuts; all the girls had square bangs. A few of the luckier girls owned white socks with large holes.

"What did you learn in school today?" my mother sometimes asked in the late afternoon as we made our way along the edge of a ricefield, looking for vines to put into a soup.

"We learned to stand to one side when a teacher passes and to bow our heads as low as we can."

"Good," my mother said. "That's important."

Another time I said, "We learned how to sit two to a chair so that our rear ends won't hurt."

"Don't they have enough chairs? We did our learning on benches."

"Benches would be better," I agreed.

Our teacher's name was Chompoo, which means *rose apple*, but we had to call her "Khun Kru," the words that mean *teacher*. She had been the teacher at that school for as long as anyone could remember. She had taught nearly everyone in our village.

"Hello, Khun Kru," people greeted her wherever she went, standing to the side as she passed. These greetings went along with her as surely as her teacher's uniform, made of khaki, and her umbrella, which she carried to ward off the sun, even on overcast days.

"Students," she asked us one morning, "what is the purpose of education? Why do you come here every day?"

She answered her own question. We knew already that the questions she asked us were not to make us think about answers, but to prepare us for her explanations.

"You are all here to learn that you're nothing special," Khun Kru Chompoo told us. "Have you learned that basic lesson yet? Look at yourselves. Look! Compare your shirt with the other shirts in your row. Compare your haircuts. Compare them! Are they the same? Of course they're the same. Every one of you is equal. How can things that are equal be special? Repeat after me."

"How can things that are equal be special?" we asked. Khun Kru's technique of making us repeat her own words had trained us to make sure we listened.

"Time for a quiz," she announced.

Khun Kru Chompoo was famous for her quizzes. The questions on her quizzes often had no correct answers. We had to guess what she was thinking.

"This quiz is about duty," she said. "What's your most important duty? That is the question. Here are the answers. A. To serve the temple." She gave us a long look. "B. To serve the village. C. To serve the country. D. To serve your parents. E. To serve yourself. There you are. Five choices. That's enough. Repeat the five choices to me."

We repeated. Then Khun Kru called on Nop, a fidgety boy who was hoarse. Khun Kru's technique while we answered was to look off in the distance impatiently. She never seemed to notice Nop's fidgeting.

"I choose my parents," said Nop at last, even more hoarsely than usual.

"Which choice is that?"

"Choice D."

"To serve your parents?"

"Choice D. To serve my parents," Nop stammered.

"That's fine," said Khun Kru Chompoo. "But what about the monks at the temple? They help everyone. Do you think your family is more important than everyone else?"

She shook her head and called on Nid, a girl in the corner, as Nop slumped back into his seat.

"I choose to serve the temple," said Nid confidently.

"Oh, you do?" said Khun Kru. "And you'd ignore the village? Don't forget, the village supports the temple. If the village disappears, the temple disappears along with it. Come on, students. Who can give me a good answer?"

Someone else said it was best to serve the village. Khun Kru asked why our little village was more important than the whole country. So when she called on me, I said that of course I would serve the country. We are Thai, and everyone around us is Thai, too, I said with great confidence. Khun Kru shook her head and explained that the family is the basic unit in society, and if we don't build strength in our families, then society would fall, and Thailand would fall along with it. Didn't I love my parents? she asked me, once again shaking her head.

I sat down and waited for her to look away so that I could adjust my rear end on the chair.

Khun Kru swept her eyes around the room. "Only one answer is left," she said. "How many of you chose 'E. To serve yourself'?"

None of us had.

"Why in the world not?" asked Khun Kru Chompoo.

"It's selfish," somebody said.

"We're not special," Nop said in his hoarse, fidgety voice.

"If we take care of other people, other people will take care of us," said a girl in the front who could usually guess the correct answers.

Khun Kru sighed and spent a moment rubbing her forehead. "Students," she said, "Look. Part of serving yourself is respecting your parents. Another part is making merit at the temple. Another part is developing your village. And doing all these things will make Thailand grow stronger and stronger."

She stared directly at each one of us. "Of course you begin with yourself. You serve yourself, but you don't do it selfishly. Don't you see? This is a perfect example of 'First things first.'" She stopped and said, "Repeat that."

"First things first!" we all said.

Khun Kru put her hand back up to her forehead and spoke softly. "Listen, students. I'll be retiring soon.

I don't know who will take over for me, but one thing I'm afraid of is that you won't learn what I'm teaching you, and the new teacher will think that I wasn't doing my job. How would that make me feel? So I'm trying to teach you better than I ever taught any classes before. Better than I taught your parents and your older brothers and sisters. Not that I taught them poorly. But don't you appreciate my hard work? I'm doing it for your sakes, you know."

She stopped for a moment and winced. "Students. You've given me a headache. It's even worse than the one you gave me yesterday. I want you to sit quietly and think about all the things I've taught you this morning while I go and drink some hot tea."

"Hot tea!" we all said. We stood at attention as she left the room.

Khun Kru Chompoo took the rest of the day off.

STAIRCASE

B efore I was born, my father was one of a team of men who built houses up and down through our village and over into the next one as well.

"Those were the days," my father often says, though he always adds, "but then again, so are these." Back then, houses were all made of wood, and they were built up off the ground on tall posts. Life was predictable for him, and he liked that.

Then along came cement blocks and concrete.

People in our village dreamed of owning new, modern houses. They became optimistic. They began building even if they didn't have enough money to finish a whole house.

People bought as much concrete as they could afford. Some families put up only a foundation and then waited to save enough money to add on more of the house. Some built only two walls and maybe part of a third. Our favorite belonged to Uncle Song, who put up a staircase that led up to nothing. Then he ran out of money.

"Well begun is half done," our parents said as they took us on walks down our lane past those houses. But soon the droughts that everyone now knows so well had spread to our village. Money was harder to come by. People's thoughts turned from finishing their houses to trying to salvage the rice crop. Even today, our lane is full of half-finished houses—good beginnings scattered around through our village.

My father switched over to his next career, making small bamboo tables, which people sat on when neighbors came by, as they so often did in our village. This career was natural for him, since the area behind our house was full of bamboo. We called it the Bamboo Garden. My sister and I liked to find new sprouts and keep track of them as they grew. We ran our hands over the stalks, which grew straight and fast, unlike houses.

Whenever my father took me back to the garden to cut bamboo for his tables, he stopped sawing for a moment and said, "Someday, Het, we're going to build a house for you and your family, right here on this spot." He surveyed the site proudly. "Those are going to be the days, too." He had another site picked out for my sister.

My father sat under our house making his bamboo tables. After he had finished a half dozen or so, he loaded them onto a cart and wheeled them around through our village. The tables on the cart were piled high up over his head.

My father could make tables better than anyone in our village or the next one over, which were the only two places I knew of. And he could balance the tables up on the cart so that they never slipped off.

But he was not much of a salesman. He used to wheel the cart down the lane, then stop at somebody's house. He sat there talking about anything except the big pile of tables parked out in the lane. Then he gave his trademark, "Stop by anytime," and he went back out to the cart.

"Why didn't you try to sell any?" I asked as we pushed on down the lane. "Their table was all cracked and wobbly!"

"That's exactly why I didn't say anything." He pushed on a ways before he explained. "Anybody with a worn-out table would love to have a new one. That's human nature. They know I make tables. If they could afford one, they would have brought it up themselves." He stopped the cart at the next house. "There's no point in making people feel bad." We went in and sat on the next family's rickety table, and the next family's, too, after that.

Uncle Song, who had gone off to the city hoping to earn the money he needed to build an upstairs for his staircase, eventually found a new job for my father. A furniture store in the city contracted my father to build hardwood tables. He worked under our house with the bamboo tables all around. They gave him inspiration, he said. Besides, neighbors stopped by every evening, and those unsold tables gave them plenty of well-built places to sit down.

As for Uncle Song, he never was able to make the money he dreamed of in the city, and that was fine with us kids. We loved playing around on his staircase. We made up games that we never would have thought of if those stairs had just been part of a house.

Like almost everything else in our village, that staircase has a story behind it, one that says something about the people who live here. When Uncle Song was getting ready to build his house, he knew he didn't have enough money even to finish the whole staircase. So he went around to people in our village. "I have enough cement to build half a staircase," he told them. "Should I build it half-high or half-wide?" It was a question people had never thought about before, so they considered their answers carefully. They listened in on other people's opinions, too. Many of these people, remember, were owners of new houses that consisted of nothing more than half a wall here and some unfinished posts over there. So the question made good sense to them. And soon two groups had formed. The half-high group said that a solid foundation was the key to success in the world. The half-widers said no, a narrow pathway has fewer distractions.

It became a great debate in our village. "Which side are you on," people were asking, "half-high or half-wide?" They studied Uncle Song carefully to see which kind he favored.

Uncle Song said later that he was never more popular than during the time of the great staircase debate. Men went to him and offered their prized chickens, if only he would build his staircase half-high. "Nothing illegal," they told him. "I just want to prove a point to my brother." Other men said that if he built the staircase half-high, they'd never hear the end of it from their wives. "Half-wide," they whispered to him, "and you'll have your choice of next year's piglets."

For days, no one talked about anything other than stairs. But here's the thing about our village: half-high or half-wide wasn't important to us at all. Nobody cares that much about staircases. Life is slow here, though, and those were dry times. For all the offers of chickens and piglets, people were just happy to have something to talk about besides the stalks of rice wilting in the fields and the dust settling down on that year's crop of undersize mangoes. Uncle Song's staircase debate swept through our village like a soft morning rain, and we made it a point to collect every drop.

Soon the offers to Uncle Song changed. A wife and husband whose own house-building plans had stalled came to him first. "We know what it's like to be short of construction materials," they told him one night.

"We're willing to give you two steps from our own staircase if you think it might help."

My grandparents gave him a bag of cement they'd been saving toward a new staircase for their old wooden house. "We've been using a ladder to get upstairs all our lives," they said. "There's no reason for us to switch to stairs now."

Uncle Song protested, but contributions kept coming in. For a while there, he couldn't take an afternoon nap without waking to find that a half bag of cement had been left by his hammock.

Finally the village headman came by. "Listen," he said. "This is a golden opportunity for Slippery Stream Banks Village. If we play this staircase debate right, we can turn it into an example of the whole village joining together, one that will be remembered for generations to come." And he donated two more bags to the cause.

At last Uncle Song announced that he was ready to start building. So much time had been spent debating his staircase that a large crowd turned out to hear his decision. People who tell this story say that the crowd was split into two groups, with the half-widers holding up banners and the half-high group leading cheers. Uncle Song stood up between them.

"I've made a compromise," he said, speaking softly so that the groups would have to edge closer together. "I'd like a wide staircase, but of course I'd also like it to lead somewhere." He paused for a moment to allow the crowd time to stir.

"As it turns out," he went on, "so many of you have donated cement that I now have enough to build a staircase and a half. I thank you all for your kindness, but that's more than any house needs." Another pause, and again the crowd stirred. "So here's what I plan to do. I'd like to take all of your donations and build stairs that are both high enough and wide enough to—"

But the crowd cut him off with a cheer. "We won!" the half-high group shouted. "No, we did!" the half-wide group shouted right back. Uncle Song held up his hands, but it took the headman himself to quiet them down.

"Listen," he said, even as the banners began sagging. "Nobody won. Or I should say, everybody won. This is a proud moment for Slippery Stream Banks Village. We're taking these materials that so many of you contributed out of the goodness of your Slippery Stream Banks hearts, and we're not building a staircase here at all."

Once again, the crowd stirred. Even after they were quiet, the headman paused; years of making crucial speeches to our village had taught him the importance of timing. "Instead," he said finally, "we're taking them down to replace the old steps that lead up to the temple. Now who's going to help us rebuild?"

There was a moment of confusion, and then a new cheer went up. Within minutes the crowd had moved off down the lane, happy to have the great debate over and ready to get back to being lifelong friends. And it turned out that we had more than enough cement for the job at the temple. Those steps wound up being built so wide that whole families could walk right up and enter the temple together.

But plenty of cement was left over. Soon the crowd made its way back to Uncle Song's site and built the staircase that still stands there, the staircase that leads up to nothing.

And those were the stairs that became famous. The headman told the story behind them while showing them to visitors from neighboring villages. Parents stopped in the lane with their children. "That just shows you what can be accomplished when we all pitch in to help," they said.

One day as my father and I were out pushing the cartful of tables, piled high up over our heads, a family stood in the lane, admiring the staircase.

"You'll be hearing stories about that for the rest of your life," the father was telling his son just as we came along.

The son, a boy even younger than I was, looked in. "But it doesn't go anywhere," he said.

"Doesn't go anywhere?" said the father. "Well, that's the point, son."

"That's right," said the mother. "It doesn't go any-where now. But one day it will lead to the upstairs of a house made from years of hard work and patience."

"Optimism and hope, son. That's what you can learn from this staircase."

"Oh," said the boy, who was turned around, looking up at our cartful of tables.

We said hello to that family and admired the staircase along with them. Then we went on down the lane. As we pushed away, the mother was saying, "Just imagine the upstairs that would go with such a staircase."

"Ah," said the father, "what a feeling it would give you to finish a project like that!"

As it turned out, of course, Uncle Song never did.

THE PLACE

My father was a slow, careful worker who spent hours each day making tables. But even he had his diversions. He played cards. He checked the bamboo in the garden. And every so often he took out his net and his gun and went fishing.

He pulled on a pair of galoshes, and the two of us headed out through our village. That was an odd sight, those black rubber boots making their way down our dusty gray lane. My father walked faster in those boots than he normally did. He took longer strides.

"This way," he called back over his shoulder. "The fish are getting impatient." I could tell by the strides and by the sound of his voice that he was just as happy as I was.

He led me down a path that veered off from our lane, and we followed that out through the ricefields to the stream.

"Where should we try our luck?" my father asked.

"Let's go to The Place," I said as I trotted along keeping up.

My father's strides got even longer. "All right. The Place it is."

We always went to The Place. We followed the stream to the next bend, and then to the bend after that. We crossed a rickety footbridge and sat in the shade of the trees on the opposite bank. That was The Place. The two bends, the trees, and the footbridge seemed to isolate us from the world, which to me consisted of our village and the lane that led to the next one.

"Not many kids are as lucky as you," my father said as we got ready. "You were born here in Slippery Stream Banks Village with a whole lifetime of fishing at The Place to look forward to. Don't forget that." Then he tossed his net out over the water, pulled it back, and tossed it out again.

Fishing had its purpose, of course. We needed to eat. But to me, a boy who lived in a house with no plumbing, it was a chance to get away with my father and learn what I took to be the ways of the world.

In our family, the daily chores took so long that we didn't have time for much else. Everything had a purpose, and everything was done by hand. This was true for all the families in our village.

My parents started every morning by making a fire to cook over. My sister and I pushed a cartful of jugs to the public well and waited our turn to fill them. Then we pushed the heavy cart back.

In our free time, we found branches and broke kindling for the next day's fire. My mother mashed chilies and garlic for food. My father steamed sticky rice by the kettle, then soaked the next batch. We did all these things cheerfully, and why not? It was the only way we knew. It was the way that we saw all around us.

"Why are we bringing the gun?" I asked the first time we went to The Place. "Are we going to shoot the fish in the stream?"

"We couldn't do that," said my father. "That would give us a bad reputation, and the rest of the fish wouldn't want to be caught by us anymore. No, the gun is for snakes."

"We're going to shoot snakes?"

"Not that, either. But snakes are afraid of guns, Het. If the snakes see we have one, they won't come near us. We can sit on the bank and fish peacefully."

He often held out the gun in plain view as we came over the footbridge. "Ask me if I brought the gun," he would whisper to me.

"Did you bring it along?" I said.

"Louder, Het. And say 'the gun.'"

"Did you bring the gun, Dad?"

"I have the gun right here," he called out over the stream. "Here I come with the gun." He gave me a wink and held the gun low, down where the snakes could get a good look. "That ought to do it," he said.

He had been bitten on the foot by a snake as a boy, my grandmother said, and his toes had swollen up dangerously. That made him cautious about snakes for the rest of his life, and cautious on my behalf, too. One time after I had seen him shake the gun at some bushes, I said, "I guess life would be perfect if it weren't for snakes."

To my surprise, he disagreed. "If we didn't have snakes to watch out for, we'd just worry more about scorpions. Or stray dogs or mosquitoes. So we might as well worry about snakes."

One day on our way to The Place my father stopped short, just as we came to the footbridge. I caught up and saw why. I was expecting to see a snake; instead, we saw a man down in the shade, fishing the waters of The Place.

Even then I was old enough to know the rules of the stream. Every family had its own place, just as my father and I had ours. The stream was not big, and some of those places were not far apart—maybe on one side of a tree trunk and another. But everyone knew where they were. And to fish in someone else's place brought bad luck not only to you, but to the rest of the stream, besides.

I was sure the man came from another village because I knew everyone in mine, and no one in my village would have broken the rules of the stream.

"Who is it?" I said. "What's he doing down there?"

My father's fingers were gripping the butt of the gun. He was taking deep breaths.

"Let's do something," I said.

My father did. He took one last deep breath and strode out over the footbridge. He was wearing those rubber galoshes. The intruder looked up.

"Hello, friend!" called my father. He dropped down to the bank. "How's the water been treating you?" My father was smiling so widely that I stopped in surprise on the footbridge and watched everything from above.

The man smiled back. "Not so good. As stingy a patch of water as I've ever seen."

"Nothing?"

"No fish. Had a couple of snakes after me, though."

He tossed out his net and pulled it back empty.

"Mind if I give you some friendly advice?" said my father. I blinked in disbelief. "Look where you're standing. Why don't you try moving this way a bit and aiming your net farther downstream?"

"It couldn't hurt," said the man. This time when he pulled in his net, I saw the silver flash of a fish inside.

"Our dinner," I thought to myself on the footbridge.

"Well, thank you," said the man. "I can feel my luck changing already."

My father and I went on down the stream, past all the places that were claimed by our village, and found a new pool to cast into.

"Why didn't you kick that guy out?" I asked.

"Don't think about him anymore. Let's fish."

"He was catching our dinner!"

"I said, no more about that."

We cast out our net and brought in some fish of our own—bigger than the one the intruder had caught, I pointed out.

My father put down the net. "Think for a minute. Have you ever seen anyone get angry down here? Have you ever seen anyone get jealous?"

"No," I said.

"This stream is our food source. Fish can feel anger, you know. It works its way into the water."

I felt my ears burning. I looked down at the stream.

"It's a kind of water pollution," my father went on. "And don't pout. Pouting's a kind of pollution itself."

On our way home, though, it was my father who looked stern. We went straight to the house of our village headman.

"No names," said the headman.

"No," said my father. "But I know who he is. I know what village he comes from."

The headman smoked as my father told him the story. His cigarettes were yellowed and loose, with tobacco slipping out of the casing.

He let out a cloud of yellow-gray smoke when my father talked about giving the intruder advice. I was sure he would give my father a good scolding.

But the headman was nodding. "You did the right thing, of course. That ought to earn some good fishing days for the whole village. Now my job is to make sure the intruder doesn't come back." He puffed away thoughtfully; then he looked down at me. "What would you do if you were the headman?"

I had always thought that a child had no right talking to someone as important as a village headman. But he had asked me a direct question.

"I'd put a curse on their village," I said.

"The whole village? He's just one man."

"That's what happened to me. One morning I was late for school, and the teacher punished the whole class. Everyone was mad at me. Now I get to school early every morning."

The headman smiled at my father. "He may have the makings of a headman himself."

"Our teacher punishes the whole class all the time," I said proudly.

Then the headman stood talking to my father. Some of the cigarette shavings dropped down on my head. Finally the headman reached down and brushed them off. "You learned a lot today, didn't you?" he said. He lit a new yellowed cigarette as we left.

In the lane going home, I walked beside my father, whose strides were much shorter now.

"There's one thing I don't understand," I said.

"What's that, Het?"

"Why did you give that intruder such good advice? Why couldn't you just say hello and walk past?"

My father laughed. "Well, I have to admit. I cheated. That wasn't my best advice. That was just something that anybody should know. He didn't seem to have any idea what he was doing."

"What's your best advice, Dad?"

But my father shook his head. "Oh, no. It doesn't come as easy as that. You'll have to find some things out for yourself, just like I did. Especially if you're planning on becoming a headman."

After that his strides became longer, and I trotted along home beside the galoshes.

RIVALRY!

Just upstream from us was Slippery Stream Bed Village. When I was still a young boy, that village chose a new headman, and our headman invited him over for a welcoming tour. Naturally, the tour ended with the staircase that led up to nothing.

We didn't know much about that visiting headman. Word had it, though, that he was a bit proud. "Uppity," is how some people put it. Proud of his village, he was, and proud of his position as well.

"That may be," said our headman. "But we'll receive him as graciously as we receive any visitor. No prejudging. Remember, that's one of our village's mottoes."

But even our headman could not keep pride from slipping into his own voice as they approached the staircase. By then he knew just where to stop in order to give his guest the most impressive view. He stood in the exact right spot that morning and worked his way through the staircase story. He knew when to pause as he told it, too.

The visiting headman nodded. "A staircase, you say. Well, so it is. Mind if I climb to the top?"

"Not at all," our headman told him, pleased that his guest showed so much interest. "Right this way!"

But on the first step the visitor turned back to him and said, "I just want to see what kind of view I can get of my own village from up here."

Our headman staggered when he heard this, for the visitor had just committed a serious breach of headman etiquette. It was well known that a visiting headman should pay undivided attention to his host's village and should not make any mention of his own village unless specifically asked to do so by his host.

This visitor marched right up the stairs, though, not even commenting on their width or workmanship, then stopped on the next-to-last step. He took a deep breath and looked out over the fields to his village.

"Ah," he said. "Yes! You can see the roof of our temple from here!" He beamed out across the ricefields. "And look! You'll have a perfect view of my new office complex, too. Did I tell you about that yet? It's going to be magnificent!"

By this time our own headman had grown light-headed and even, I've been told, had to brace himself against the side of the staircase. So he was not prepared for what happened next. The visitor, satisfied now, did not look at the view of our village. Instead, he swept his eyes from his own village right back to the top step of the staircase.

"Why, what's this?" he said, stooping down for a closer look—and then giving a start and nearly toppling down to the ground.

He regained his balance and came straight down the steps. "Of all the nerve!" he spouted. "I've never been so humiliated in all my days as a headman! Why, I'm humiliated officially! I'm humiliated on behalf of Slippery Stream Bed Village!" He turned to walk off, and our headman came after him, asking him what was the matter.

"No, no," the visitor said. "Don't see me off. I can find my way home from here. Thank you very much!" He stomped off but then turned back again. "I'll have you know that this is a serious breach of Slippery Stream etiquette!" This time he stomped off for good.

As it turned out, that headman's visit and his sudden departure had widespread and long-lasting effects on our village.

The first thing that happened was that our own headman recovered from his daze and decided to climb the staircase himself. He stood there looking around, and even saw the visitor heading away, still stomping, through the ricefields. The visitor was almost all the way home before our headman looked down and saw that something had been painted on the top step of the staircase.

A message.

The second thing that happened was that I decided I had to learn how to read, for no one would tell me what that painted message said! I climbed up there, but I couldn't make out the words. I asked the older boys, but they said—in kind of an uppity way, it seemed to me—"If you're not old enough to read it, I guess you're not meant to know what it says."

None of the boys my age could read it, and our fathers wouldn't tell us, either. "That's a sensitive issue right now, boys," they all said, then rushed off to a meeting with the headman.

Our mothers claimed to know nothing. "Oh, there's a message?" they said, even though we had seen our fathers whispering urgently with them before heading off.

My friends and I spent hours that day trying to learn the secret of the message. To some people, that may not seem like a very long time. But remember, not much ever happened in our village, so when something finally did, news spread in no time, and excitement spread right along with it. The message on the staircase was the biggest thing that had happened in our young lives, and not being able to find out what it said was the worst. We watched groups of older kids huddling together, talking it all over, but we were on the outside. We finally gave up and went home.

I was up in a mango tree beside our house, sulking, when a group of older boys walked down the lane. Boy, they looked happy. "I'll show them," I was thinking as they walked out of sight. "Someday I'll become headman, and whenever I have a secret, I won't tell them. Then they'll be sorry." The idea of getting even with them seemed so satisfying that I was almost glad I didn't know what the staircase message said.

But I forgot about the future when my father appeared, on his way home from the meeting. At that very same moment, Uncle Song came down the lane from the opposite direction, returning from yet another failed business trip to the city.

"Not a thing," he told my father. "I thought I had something going with a man who wants to raise eels, but—"

"Not now," my father said. And he told Uncle Song about the message.

"On my staircase? You're kidding! What does it say?"

My father looked around—but he didn't look up.

"It says, 'Staircase—Pride of the Slippery Stream Region.'"

Uncle Song winced. "Pride," he said. "That's not good."

"No, it isn't."

Uncle Song was shaking his head. "Who wrote it?"

"We don't know. I was just looking for you. We're preparing to set up an investigative committee." And they went down the lane again, back to the house of the headman.

I stayed up in the tree until they were gone. "Pride of the Slippery Stream Region." I memorized those words, then raced down the lane to tell all my friends.

And I found them—racing to tell me. It turned out that one of the older boys had told them, in exchange for their slingshots and a week's supply of small stones.

"We knew before you did!" they told me.

"Maybe," I said. "But I didn't have to give up my slingshot!"

We never did find out who wrote that message, although for weeks no one talked about anything else. Paint samples were taken, and my uncles dusted the staircase once for fingerprints, then again for toeprints, but the mystery grew deeper.

And that leads to the third thing that happened. A new message appeared on the top step. Not right away, of course. Change takes its time in our village. Months passed, or even years—no one is quite sure, and people argue about it even today—with that same message up there.

And then one morning, one of my classmates came sprinting down the lane. "There's a new message!" he was shouting, and just like that, the mystery deepened.

It shows something about the pace of life in our village, I think, that a wait of months—or perhaps years—was just about right for something new to come up. It took us that long to talk about the old thing from every possible angle, and to tell everyone what we had heard and from whom, and then to tell it again and again until we had memorized the exact words of everyone else in the village. To us, that's how an event was remembered.

The new message read,

Danger—Don't climb up to the top.

Nobody could guess who wrote it, and to tell the truth, nobody really wanted to know, because then we would have had to find something else to talk about.

We stretched out the discussions; twists were thrown in.

"The paint's the same color as the first time," one man said when a group gathered at my family's house one night.

"But the handwriting looks different."

"Well, anybody's handwriting is bound to change when you're writing in paint on the top of a staircase."

"Here's what I don't get," said a woman who lived out by the temple. "This message was written as a warning, yet anyone who wants to read it has to climb all the way to the top—and according to the message, that's dangerous!"

"You're right," someone else said. "And the person who wrote it had to climb all the way up there himself."

"Or herself," someone added, and the mystery deepened once more.

Every few years while I was growing up, a new message appeared on the top step of the staircase. It became a regular feature of life in our village, like a memorable windstorm or an especially sweet crop of mangoes. Sometimes we weren't even sure when the latest message had been written, for no one climbed the staircase for weeks at a time, and when somebody finally did, there it was. The messages created a stir when they appeared, but they brought satisfaction, too. They reassured us that, whatever troubles we had, life in our village was going along as it should.

But a fourth thing happened after that proud headman's visit, and it is a story that children here will be told for as long as there is a Slippery Stream Banks Village.

That headman stomped back home and immediately called a meeting. He told his fellow Slippery Stream Bed villagers about the insulting message he had seen and announced that they must take revenge. He had a plan ready, he said, and together they would carry it out.

The proud headman's plan was to build a dam. The Slippery Stream Bed villagers carried leaves and branches and baskets of soil down to the stream, and soon the water stopped flowing past our village.

Our headman went with a team of villagers and a gift of ripe banana buds to apologize, but their headman would not even receive them. "The damage is done," they were told, and the group returned home to decide what to do next.

"We could put a curse on that dam," someone suggested. Again a group had gathered at our house, and I sat outside the circle, listening.

"I don't think so," someone else said. "Our message caused the problem in the first place, and the curse might come right back to haunt us."

"What about the provincial authorities? This affects other villages, you know."

"It would be years before the province got to it. Why, my grandfather's still waiting for a ruling on a crate of watermelons that was stolen from him back before he got married!"

"You're right. We've got to handle this ourselves. Why don't we wait until the wood dries, then burn the dam out?"

"No, no. They water it down every morning. And besides, they've got the thing under twenty-four-hour watch."

"Well, we'd better do something soon, or we'll be back to the days of the rivalry."

The rivalry. Everyone nodded and went silent. Even I was old enough to know about the rivalry, though it had happened years before I was born. It had started with a soccer game, a "friendly," between the two villages. The game was supposed to be all in good fun, and there was laughter as the two sides gathered to decide on the rules for the friendly encounter. But problems emerged at that meeting. Each village wanted to play on its own field, for one thing—and each wanted to bring its own ball. A suggestion was made to hold the game out in the ricefields between the two villages, with a ball they borrowed from the district sporting authority, but the headmen at the time worked out a different compromise. The first half would be played with our ball on the Slippery Stream Bed Village field, they decided, and the second half would be played with their ball on ours.

Everyone seemed satisfied with that plan, and the game itself was friendly enough, with hard, clean play and good-natured cheering from the sidelines. But a new problem came up. The game ended in a tie—and no one could agree on where to play the overtime, or which side's ball they should use. As the argument grew, a storm blew in and rained out the rest of the game.

To this day, grandfathers who played in that game tell their versions of what happened. "That game wasn't a tie," they insist. "It's still not over! We're going to beat those guys yet!"

The two sides never could agree on conditions for an overtime, and the soccer game remained forever unsettled. That's how the rivalry started. It was a quiet rivalry, of course—a friendly one. Women from our village who made an especially good batch of soup might take some over to their village. They were being friendly, sure—but were they perhaps showing off a bit, too? And when Slippery Stream Bed Village School sent students over to perform traditional dances for us—didn't those friendly smiles say, "Look how graceful we are"?

That's what people were remembering as they sat under our house that night. They went home still scratching their heads over how to deal with the dam. They were worried about how long we could get by without fish, yet satisfied that at least they had something new to discuss.

The next day our headman called us together. He had just started speaking when Uncle Song turned up.

"Sorry to interrupt," he said, bowing to the headman, "but this may be important." With the headman's permission, he turned to the crowd. Uncle Song had wandered down to the dam that morning for a chat with the guards on duty. A friendly chat, it had been, but now he was full of excitement.

"The fish on their side of the stream are nudging at the dam," he reported as the crowd drew closer. "Water's already trickling through. You see what that means? The fish don't want to live near that village. They want to get back here to live near us!"

The excitement spread quickly, as it always does, and this time I was in on it. In groups of twos and threes that day, we all managed to get down to the dam for a look. Sure enough, the fish were gathered there, and sure enough, they were trying to break through. We returned home not only proud but even a little bit smug.

That very night, the dam gave way. The water burst through and returned to our part of the stream. For months, that was all we talked about, that even the fish couldn't stand living on that side of the dam—even they knew where life was better. And how plump those fish were, now that they were back on our side. How healthy! Those fish were natural proof of what we had always suspected. We beamed when we talked about that; as we watched the fish surge through the water, we took deep happy breaths of our air.

For months, or even years, we went on believing all that, holding our heads high as we walked down our lane. But later, about the time the second message was appearing on the staircase, we learned what really did happen. It turned out that the people of Slippery Stream Bed Village didn't want a dam in the stream any more than we did. They had had it with their uppity headman, and they decided to use his orders to build the dam as a way of getting him out.

They built that dam solid, as he had instructed, but they secretly packed it full of fish bait. Of course, the fish ganged up there, trying to get at all that food, and once they did, the dam began to give way. When it broke, the angry villagers got rid of the headman, even before he could start building his office complex. Their new headman was a good, fair man who proved it by coming straight to our village and asking for a personal tour to the staircase.

Nowadays when people in our village tell that story, they agree that it was a clever idea, packing the dam full of bait, and that the proud headman had gotten what he deserved. They say they are satisfied that things turned out as they did. But others may not be so sure. Even today—you can see it in their faces as they listen—many people here wish they could have gone on believing that it all happened because of the natural goodness of our village, and because those fish simply preferred to plump themselves up and come down here to live out their days in our calm, quiet—and less prideful—part of the Slippery Stream.

OLD MR. POTE

Old Mr. Pote used to sit in the grocery, making small talk with people who came to buy fish sauce and garlic. He helped us kids fix our kites. He came down after school to keep goal, then gave us pointers on how we could kick our old soccer ball past him.

Old Mr. Pote was not all that old. But "Old" is what everyone called him.

There were reasons for that. He had a stiff way of moving, even when he was in goal. He sighed often. He talked of events that had taken place in our village back before any of the grandparents had been born. He called it "old knowledge," though there was no way to know if those stories were true or if he was just making things up as he went.

And, as my grandmother liked to point out, Old Mr. Pote had never been married.

The grandparents in our village were convinced that there was an order to life, an order that included being parents.

"Marry young, you hear?" they told us. "Marry young and have kids. Then you can grow old in peace." We nodded when we heard that, glad that the future was so far away.

Still, even I knew there was something that set Old Mr. Pote apart. Just what was it about him?

I first noticed it one morning when I was tending Uncle Saam's oxen. I left them in a grassy field and slipped off to watch the flow of the stream. Under the footbridge sat Old Mr. Pote.

"Little mouse," he called to me. "What's your name, little mouse?"

"My name's Het."

"Well, Mr. Het. I've got something to tell you."

"What is it?"

"It's a secret."

"Oh, I like secrets." I stepped closer to him.

Old Mr. Pote smiled and said nothing.

"I'm ready to listen," I told him.

"I can see that. But this is a secret."

"You said you had something to tell me."

"Oh, I do! I've got something wonderful! But"—he hesitated—"if I told you this secret, you'd think I was mad."

"No, I wouldn't. I promise. And I wouldn't tell anybody, either. I'd keep your secret forever."

Old Mr. Pote shook his head. "You're a good boy, Het. I can see that. But my mind is made up. It just wouldn't do to tell you."

I tried my best to show my disappointment, but Old Mr. Pote wouldn't be swayed.

"I'm sorry, Het. But now I need to ask you to do me a favor."

"What is it?"

"I want you to promise not to tell anybody else that I've got a secret. Can you promise me that?"

Since I didn't know what the secret was, it didn't seem like much of a promise. I said, "All right. I promise I won't tell."

Old Mr. Pote gave a huge sigh of relief. "Thank goodness. You had me worried there, Het." Then he smiled at me. "I just want you to know that I trust you."

"Well, thank you." I excused myself and went back to the oxen.

That conversation stayed so fresh in my mind that for three nights it took the place of my dreams. Then it settled down until one morning I again met Old Mr. Pote.

A shelter had been built by the side of our lane, and he was sitting there one Sunday as I went by on my way to climb trees near the school. In our village, spending a Sunday morning in that shelter was as normal a thing as a person could do.

"Little mouse," he called out as I passed.

"I'm Het."

"I know that." He lowered his voice. "Do you remember your promise?"

"I remember."

"And—have you kept it?"

"Oh, yes. I haven't told anyone."

Again he gave a sigh of relief, even bigger than the one he had given at the stream. "I knew I could trust you. You know, I didn't really have to ask if you'd kept your promise. I could see it in your eyes that you had. I could see it in your ears! You have honesty written all over you, Het."

"Thank you." I watched as he closed his own eyes, full of relief. "Are you sure you can't tell me the secret?"

"Oh, I wish I could. I would love to tell someone. Especially you, Het. It would mean so much to me. But with a secret like this, I have to be careful. Even with someone as honest and trustworthy as you are. Because if only one other person knew about this secret—if anyone even suspected—why, that person would think I was crazy." He shook his head. "No, Het. I'm sorry. If I had a run-of-the-mill secret, you'd be the first one to know. But with a secret like this—well, as I said, I have to be careful."

Other times when I saw Old Mr. Pote, he just raised his eyebrows at me, as if he were asking a question. I gave him a quick nod. He let out his sigh, then sat back.

One day Old Mr. Pote came down with a fever. He lay listlessly outside his house in a hammock, and I decided to go see him. I thought that if I let him know I was keeping the promise, safe as ever, it might give him a lift.

But Old Mr. Pote's house was crowded with people. I could see the straps holding the hammock between two jackfruit trees, but I couldn't see him.

"All of us feel as if we are his family," my grandmother said as we watched crowds of villagers come by. "I suppose that may be one advantage of not having children."

Finally some doctors from the city arrived at Old Mr. Pote's. He waved them away from his hammock.

"I appreciate your coming," he said hoarsely. "But I've got everything I need."

"If we can just check you over," a doctor said politely. "Maybe we could prescribe a good medicine."

"Someone just brought me hot ginger soup. What medicine could be better than that?"

The doctors tried several more times before giving up. And that night, the crowd stayed by the hammock, fanning mosquitoes away from Old Mr. Pote.

"I did it," he finally sighed. "It's safe now. I kept you. Success."

Those were the last words Old Mr. Pote ever spoke.

Everybody crowded into the temple for his funeral. It was the most people in black I'd ever seen. We heard the thump of the big temple drum.

A few adults stood up and said things about Old Mr. Pote. They talked about how friendly he'd been, back when he used to sit at the grocery. They said he would always be remembered with fondness.

Then a new man stood up. He introduced himself as a garlic supplier from three villages away. He had a few strands of hair combed over his head.

"Who are we kidding here?" said the garlic supplier. "Let's face it. Old Mr. Pote was crazy! Every time I came to your village—and I'm in garlic, you know—every time I came here, he told me he had some kind of secret. Ha! The stories I could tell about him. Where was his secret? What was it? And whenever he saw me, he made me promise not to tell anyone that he'd told me. Ha! Told me what? Let's be honest here. Old Pote was a madman, and that's it!" He shook his head, laughing at his memory of Old Mr. Pote.

But no one was laughing along. There was a long silence in the temple. It was the headman who finally stood up and spoke to the garlic supplier. "No offense, sir. But if you promised Old Mr. Pote that you wouldn't tell—well, then, what are you doing now, telling us?"

People nodded at this. The garlic supplier took a step backward.

Uncle Song stood up. "Personally, sir, I can't remember Old Mr. Pote breaking any promises he ever made to me."

More people nodded. A breeze blew the hair up from the garlic supplier's head as he backed away from the crowd.

Then another man spoke. "He never once broke a promise to me, either. With all due respect, sir, will your mourners be able to say the same thing about you when you're gone?"

By now everyone was nodding and trying to talk to the garlic supplier. But he was already backing out of the temple, hurrying off down the road. As it turned out, he never came back, not even to supply us with garlic. We could see the sweat through the back of his shirt as he left.

After he was gone, more and more people stood up to talk about Old Mr. Pote.

"I can tell you," said one, "there are a lot of boys in this village who won't get the same kick out of flying a kite without Old Mr. Pote's helping hand."

An older boy stood, too. "It's going to be a long time before I play soccer again. How can I enjoy it if Old Mr. Pote isn't in goal?"

Then another man got up to speak. "As Old Mr. Pote's cousin, I believe I'm his closest relative here." He stopped and cleared his throat. "I want to tell you straight out. I promised Old Mr. Pote, too. But now that he's gone, I'm going to break my promise." Some people murmured as the man cleared his throat once again. "And out of respect for Old Mr. Pote's memory, I'd just like to ask, if you don't mind, all those who made a promise to him, would you mind breaking your promise now, and please stand?"

At first, no one moved.

"Trust me," the cousin said. "For him."

Slowly, the headman got to his feet. My uncles coughed, and then they rose, too. So did my father. Soon Khun Kru Chompoo was standing, along with the rest of the women. Children were shifting around, and they stood among the adults. At last, I stood. All of my friends, the ones who played soccer together, were standing up, too.

The cousin was looking out over the crowd, nodding slowly. "There now, you see? All these promises, and how many of you ever broke them? Not a soul! Now, I may be doing the wrong thing, exposing all the promises like this, but I just want everyone to see the lesson that Old Mr. Pote was teaching. My cousin was no madman. That wasn't his lesson at all. The lesson Old Mr. Pote taught us was trust!"

Everybody was nodding now, and even the children were murmuring, some for the first time in their lives. The headman went to the front.

"I'd just like to tell you," he said, "that Old Mr. Pote has always been one of my heroes."

Everyone nodded again, and soon voices called out.

"He was a good, honest man."

"He never did wrong by me."

"Long live the memory of Old Mr. Pote!"

A wave of good feeling passed through our temple, and the funeral broke up with farmers eager to get back their fields, mothers hugging their children, and the thumps on the big temple drum sounding louder than ever.

Everywhere we looked after that, we saw reminders of Old Mr. Pote. On the field at school, we played a new kind of soccer, with no goalkeepers. The headman named our lane after him. The grocer kept Old Mr. Pote's bench in her store, and everyone knew not to sit there.

And Old Mr. Pote's name came up again and again in village conversation.

"What do you think?" someone would ask. "Was it right for his cousin to bring it all out in the open?"

"Well, he had a right to, as family."

"You know, if he hadn't done that, I would have lived out my life thinking I was the only one."

"Admit it, though. You thought Old Mr. Pote was odd when he first made you promise, didn't you?"

"Maybe a little. Still, I would have kept it forever if it hadn't been for that day at the temple."

"Old Mr. Pote," someone would add. "We were sure lucky to have him."

And then there were sighs all around.

SAME TIME TOMORROW

U ncle Song's hobby was betting on things. He bet on card games and boxing. Well, everyone did that. But he took it further. He bet on the rain. Would it start, and if it did, when would it stop? He bet on the number of steps it took to walk from the stream to the temple, and then the number of steps it took to walk back. He bet on the number of custard apples on a tree, and the number of seeds in each piece of fruit.

He admitted all of this freely. He was proud of his betting, in fact. He boasted that he had made bets that no one else could have thought of.

"It's not any special talent," I heard him telling my mother one day. "It's just keeping your mind ready. It's like a monk keeping his mind open for new lessons to teach. Everything's useful to him because he's ready to use it. Well, I'm the same way. I look for the bet in a thing. It's an instinct, that's all. Watch. I'm looking outside right now. I bet the headman is the next one to come down the lane. And if he's not the first, I bet he isn't the second one, either."

My mother did not take that bet. But I did. And right away, my father came down the lane and into the house.

"*Chai-yo!*" I said, for I had won the first bet.

Before my father could even ask what had happened, the village headman came down the lane next. I cried out again.

"You owe me," I said to Uncle Song. "You owe me twice!"

"What's going on?" my father asked.

"We're betting," Uncle Song said. "But I bet you can't guess what our bet was."

Uncle Song loved betting on his book most of all. He carried an old hardback wherever he went, so dependably that the sweat from his palm had faded the cover from black to pale gray. He didn't read the book, though; he bet on it.

The basic game was for each of the players to choose a page number. Then someone opened the book. That's all. Whoever came closest was the winner.

There were variations, of course. Sometimes the pot grew, and there was doubling, and neighbors who stopped by joined in, too. Sometimes Uncle Song wound up playing solitaire. But always he was the center of attention.

"Double payoff when you bet your birthday," he'd announce as he sat on the table under our house. "Triple when you bet your age. Who's in? The game's on. We're playing the book here. If you're not in, you can't win."

"What's the name of that book, anyway?" someone once asked him.

"The title's worn off," Uncle Song said. "Are you in?"

His betting took him around the village. In the mornings he could be found at a table in front of our village's grocery, a one-room wooden store near the temple. By afternoon he had moved on to the shelter by the side of the road. And at night he preferred to come and sit under our house.

People who passed by sat down and joined him. "It's your day," he told them. "I can feel it. What's your play?"

There were two things about Uncle Song's betting. One was that he never won. He was especially bad at the book game. It was as if his fingers had learned the feel of each page of that book, and he could open it to any page he wanted, and he could draw more and more people into the game, and all of them won until it was time for the game's last jackpot, with the day's biggest payoff, and then he could call his own number, and when he flipped the book open, there would be his choice, and he would walk off with all the winnings.

Only that never happened. He still didn't win. And when he handed the book over to let someone else open it, he couldn't win then, either. "Not my day," he always said. "Same time tomorrow?"

He was even worse at rummy than he was at the book game. He could play all afternoon without winning a hand. "One card away," he said when someone went out. "Where was that jack of diamonds, anyhow?"

One time I saw a neighbor of ours shake his head in admiration after winning hand after hand all night. "Not his day," he said as Uncle Song headed home. "But I'll tell you. You've got to be pretty sharp to be able to lose as often as that."

It got so that the men in my village invented a system of tricks and signals to force Uncle Song to win. It was like cheating in reverse. But even that didn't work. Eventually, one of the men would get cramps in his legs, or his fingers, and throw down a winning hand in frustration.

"So you had it!" Uncle Song would say. "You had that jack all along!" And he shook his head as the hand was collected.

Then his face became brighter. "Whose deal?" he asked, always looking ahead.

So one thing about his betting was that he never won. The other thing was that he never bet for money.

That's not surprising, since no one in our village ever had much to begin with. "The best thing about being poor," my aunt said, "is that we don't have any money for my husband to lose." And she beamed at him.

Instead, he kept score. Uncle Song kept a running total in his mind at all times, and it was surprisingly accurate.

"Nice play," he'd say. "You're up forty." Or, "You got me. I was only one card away. That puts you up sixty."

Everyone was always up. The trick was to try to go down. But no one could lose to Uncle Song. And of course there was never any payoff. The points added up, the players got fed up with winning, and finally they said, "Time to cash in." That meant that they had won so much that they could no longer stand it.

"Time to cash in," they said, and Uncle Song replied, "Come back and collect your winnings tomorrow. Same time."

The next day, there they were again, trying to get the worst of Uncle Song. Overnight, the scores had gone back down to zero, and everyone had a clean slate. No one minded that he never paid off. That was just part of the game. Sometimes a man who had just said, "Time to cash in," stood up, stopped for a moment, then threw down an actual coin as a tip for Uncle Song. He'd take the coin and donate it to the temple, betting on the number of dogs he'd see on the way.

One day, on one of the hottest afternoons anybody could remember, a bigger crowd than usual had gathered at the shelter for the book game. I was on the outside of the crowd, standing on a railing, looking over shoulders and trying to stay out of the sunlight.

That was the day a man no one had seen before turned up in our village and made his way to the shelter. I heard later that he had come from another village to sell off his oxen, but those were the days of the drought, and of course no one was buying.

Like any stranger, the man was curious, and he worked his way closer and closer to the game. Before anyone knew how it happened, the stranger was sitting down across from Uncle Song.

"What's the game?" the stranger said, and he introduced himself.

"It's an honor to play with a man from your village," said Uncle Song, and he explained the book game.

"Ah, the book game," said the stranger. "You know, I've played that nearly every day of my life. And you know something? I've never won."

A stirring went through the crowd, and I nearly lost my footing on the railing.

Uncle Song nodded slowly. "So you know the game, then," he said. "What's your play?"

"I'll play my age," said the stranger. "Thirty-nine."

"And I'll play mine. Thirty-one."

Another man, the father of my friend Nop, was holding the book. "Any backers?" he asked.

Normally the crowd shouted out side bets, picking the winner or predicting the sum of the page number's digits. But now it was quiet. I could hear the men sweating.

Nop's father opened the book. He fidgeted before he finally said, "Page thirty-five."

The crowd stirred again. I worked my way around and sat on my father's shoulders. I remember that clearly, because that was the last day I was small enough to sit there.

"Double or nothing," said Uncle Song. "What's your new play?"

"I'll play my birthday this time," said the stranger. "The twenty-first."

Uncle Song looked at him. "I was born on the twenty-first myself."

The crowd stirred even more. My father kept a good hold on my ankles.

"Triple or nothing."

The stranger nodded slowly. "I've got four daughters," he said, "and today I brought three head of cattle with me. Give me forty-three."

"I've got no daughters," said Uncle Song, "and no cattle. Give me page zero."

This time, even my father stirred. I had to hold tight to his shoulders.

Nop's father gave a cough. He stood fidgeting for a moment, and then he said, "But there's no page zero in this book."

The stranger spoke up. "We'll count page zero as the inside of the cover, before page one. Agreed?"

"Agreed," said Uncle Song, and the attention swung to Nop's father.

I don't know what came over him, whether it was the heat, or the pressure of having so many sweating men straining to see him, but Nop's father had a tense look on his face that I could see clearly over the crowd. And when he snapped the book open, the oddest thing happened. The binding broke loose, and the pages flew out of the cover and down to the floor of the shelter.

For a moment everyone stared at the pages on the floor and at the cover, still in Nop's father's hands.

The stranger from the other village was the first one to speak. "The winner!" he said, and he held Uncle Song's arm up over his head the way boxers do.

A look came over Uncle Song's face then, a look of understanding and confusion mixed together. "It must be some kind of foul," he was saying, but the stranger shook his head.

"You're up," he said, and the look on Uncle Song's face changed. No one had ever said those words to him before.

He lowered his hand and said, "But I'm not up. I bet on page zero, remember? Zero pays nothing. So I still have no points."

Now the crowd stirred so much that I wound up on the shoulders of a man halfway across the circle. Everyone was talking at once, including my father, who was the last man in any crowd to show excitement. I worked my way back over to him.

Uncle Song held his hands up, asking for quiet. "There's only one way to settle this," he said. "We'll choose a page from the floor, and that will determine the winner. Are you in?"

There was nodding all around, and the stranger nodded, too.

"In," he said.

Uncle Song picked up the pages from the floor and offered them to the stranger, who dutifully looked away and then chose one.

I don't think I've ever been in a group of men who were hotter and who minded it less than those men in that shelter that day. Our eyes were wide open as we waited for the stranger to speak up.

He was taking his time, though. He looked at one side of the page he had chosen. Then he turned it over and looked at the back.

"Why," said the stranger at last, "these page numbers are worn off!"

This time the crowd stirred even more than it had before. I could swear there was a moment when I was on the floor and my father on my shoulders, and then a moment later I was sitting on the table in the center of the shelter, right between Uncle Song and the stranger.

They were looking at the page together, and I saw it clearly.

"He's right," said Uncle Song. "There are no numbers on this page at all. It looks to me like this bet's a draw."

And that's how it ended. The crowd stirred one last time, and the men found themselves outside the shelter in groups of twos and threes, talking about what they had seen from their different angles. My father and I left, too, and Uncle Song stayed talking with the stranger for so long that he never made it over to our house that night.

I guess it would make a good story if it turned out that that was the bet that cured Uncle Song, and he swore off betting forever. But that didn't happen. The next day, he was right back at it, and if anything, he was even harder to lose to than he had been before. "Not my day," he still said, only now he seemed to really mean it.

It was weeks before the men in our village talked of anything but the page-zero bet. True, nothing else happened. But as a result of that bet, Uncle Song had become kind of a hero.

"He's your uncle?" kids asked me in admiration, as they tried to stand near me. Suddenly I was being chosen much earlier as we made teams for soccer games after school.

And it wasn't long before I was under the house, asking Uncle Song if he could deal me in on a hand.

He thought about that. "Is your mother around?"

"She went off to pick limes."

"I guess we could play a quick hand. But one's the limit," he said, and he dealt.

Within minutes, Uncle Song had chalked up another effortless loss.

"You're up," he said as he collected the cards. "But I'll get you yet."

"I want to play double or nothing!"

He stopped in midshuffle. "Who in the world taught you that?"

"You did."

He raised his eyebrows. "Did I say that? Well, in that case, Het, I'll tell you a secret. Double or nothing is what turns betting for fun into gambling. The only thing you should be betting on is having some fun now and then. Your best bet is always single or nothing."

"All right. I'll take single or nothing."

"That's more like it," Uncle Song said. "Meet me here same time tomorrow." As he shuffled the cards, he was smiling, once again looking ahead.

THE SECOND TABLE

Two lanes led out of our village. One of them went to Slippery Stream Bed Village. The second one led to a wider lane that eventually joined the road that hooked up with the paved road that went into the city.

Those lanes led out of our village; they also led in. But from what we could see of the things that came in, there wasn't much reason for us to go out. Dusty old buses arrived, cluttered with chickens and sacks full of rice and old roots. Nothing new there. A supply truck, black from its own exhaust, pulled up once a month in front of the grocery. Somehow the goods had turned dusty and sun bleached before they were even delivered. And since there were never any new products, the grocer didn't bother to put them out on display. We knew all her merchandise by heart.

So we grew up believing that the rest of the world was like ours. We never imagined that the roads out of town could take us to contrasts even sharper than the rainy-season mud against the green of the ricefields or the chanting of monks against the still morning air.

Until one day.

That was the day a car arrived in our village and pulled up in front of our school. We had seen cars before, but not one up close and as shiny as this one. It was black, and the dust from the series of roads it had traveled had not stuck to it. We were too busy gaping to guess that the driver had stopped outside our village to wipe off the car and then make a dustless grand entrance.

Inside the car was a provincial councillor with members of his staff; he came with a donation to our school. Or, at least, he presented it as a donation; it was actually part of the province's budget. The students stood in two lines out front, while Khun Kru Chompoo and the headman welcomed the provincial councillor. They bowed and presented him with flowers, but we knew that he was a great man by the shiny car that he came in—and by his shoes, which were shinier yet.

He walked past us, smiling; we stared at his car. It even had tinted-black windows. The driver stood beside the car, waiting.

"Now there is a job," we were thinking. And at that moment, two rows of village children who had never been in a car forgot about "first things first" and decided to learn how to drive. Our minds filled up with new dreams for the future, even as the car's passengers made their way into the school where we learned to always be practical and patient.

Our village bought a new flag with the money we got on that day, and we put up a sign out front, showing us the name of our school. Some of that money went toward digging new toilets for the teachers. The rest went into a fund, which was kept far away from the students.

The provincial councillor did not stay long. We stood waiting in lines until he came out, and as his car pulled away, a group of us ran after it. A new thing to do in our village! The headman had climbed in the car with the provincial councillor, and I was as surprised as anyone when they stopped in front of my house.

Later I found out what had happened. Inside the school office, the provincial councillor had admired the table. It was the only piece of furniture in the room aside from some rickety chairs, making the table seem that much more impressive. Of course, my father had made that table, and the provincial councillor demanded to meet him.

"I need a table like the one in your school," the provincial councillor said at my house. "Use your best wood. Spare no expense. Make it perfect." Then he returned to his car, the headman was bowing goodbye, and the provincial councillor was off. My mother had not even had time to bring him a welcoming glass of water.

My father set right to work. He spent more time than usual sizing up wood, and the men in our village made it their business to come watch his progress. Several times my father borrowed a motorized cart and went off down one of the lanes. He returned hours later with more wood and went straight back to work.

Finally the table was finished. We admired it under our house for a day, and then my father, my uncles, and the headman rented a truck and took the table to the provincial councillor in town.

"You're making a good name for the village," Uncle Saam told my father before they rode off.

"And for yourself," added the headman, who was quick to praise his villagers, as long as the village itself had been praised first.

My father came home in the evening.

"Did you see him?" my sister and I asked. "What did he think of the table?"

"Oh, he liked it, all right," said my father, who had an odd look on his face. He went out back of the house for a bath, as if that would wash the odd look away.

When he came back to eat supper, he told us about going to town. I was a little surprised that he would tell such a grown-up story without waiting for my sister and me to go up to sleep. But he didn't seem to mind that we were sitting right there; he just hunched over his basket of sticky rice and bowl of gray soup, and he talked.

"We got in there to the provincial hall," he began. "You should see the wood in his office. Some mighty fine teak, I'll tell you." My father stopped for a minute while he chewed; I could see he was remembering the wood. Then he went on.

"Of course we had to wait for a while to go in. A provincial councillor is a busy man, busier than we can even imagine. He can't just stop what he's doing and welcome guests, the way we can around here."

Now my father spooned up some of the soup.

"We asked him to come look at the table, to see if I'd done a good enough job." This was my father's way of being modest. "But he said no, he was sure it was all right. Then we asked him if he wanted it brought in there to his office, or if he wanted to use it at home. That's when the provincial councillor changed."

"He didn't want the table?" asked my mother. There was a worried shake to her voice.

"Not that. He said there was a change in plans. He came around from his desk and sat down, right at our level. Just like we're sitting here now. Then he told us they are renovating the old temple in town, and they want to use the table out there."

"In the temple?"

"That's right."

"Well, that's an honor, then."

"It is. But remember. Since it's a temple, I can't get paid. I have to give the table to them as a donation."

My mother understood that there was no way a man from a village, like my father, could say no to someone as important as a provincial councillor. Of course, the provincial councillor would have known that, too. My mother spoke matter-of-factly. "You spent all our money on the wood for that table," she said.

My father nodded. "Of course I did. But that's not what bothers me. What bothers me is that I never had the satisfaction of knowing I was making a table for the temple."

So he made another table. There was more sizing-up wood, more neighbors stopping by to observe, more trips down the lanes in motorized carts. Whoever was giving him wood did not seem to mind that my father couldn't pay. Maybe that was because the table was going to a temple; maybe it was because everybody trusted my father.

He never mentioned his own reputation. But he made sure I knew that things like that mattered. When I walked home through the village dirty from playing at school, he said, "Everybody can see the mud on your shirt without even having to be nosy." After that I played in the mud only in back of our house, where nobody could see my walk home.

"That's more like it," he'd say when I came home without any stains. "Now let's see if we can sand down this leg."

He worked even harder on the second table than he had on the first. He was up before sunrise and worked until long after dark. During supper he sat facing the table, and he used to jump up, sand down a patch of the surface, then come back to eat, looking over his shoulder at the place he'd just sanded. More than once I heard him go downstairs late at night, knock softly somewhere on the wood, then come back up to bed, stopping a few times on the way.

"I haven't been this happy since the first time I held a piece of bamboo," he'd tell whoever was watching. Then he bent back down to work.

And I guess it was true. I never saw him more cheerful than during those days when he was making his table for the temple. He gave satisfied sighs as he wiped off his tools. He smiled when the breeze picked up tempo and beamed if a dog trotted past. He took up winking. When neighbors asked how the table was coming, he laughed from the heart and kept working.

When the second table was finished, we kept it at home for two days. Then the same truck was rented, and the men made their way back to town.

That night when my father came home, he was not beaming or winking. He had the same odd look on his face.

This time, we did not ask him any questions. We waited until he had taken his bath and come back to eat supper. He ate for a while, silently. Then when my mother refilled his soup bowl, he talked.

"Well, we pulled up at the temple," he said, just as if we had asked. "And who do you think we met there?

That's right—the provincial councillor." He said this without any emotion at all, and we did not know how to react. So we did nothing, just sat and waited for him to continue.

"It turns out that today was the day the provincial councillor made the official donation of the first table. They had a ceremony. A big crowd was there. The provincial councillor was just leaving when we pulled up with the new table."

Out of habit, my father glanced toward his workshop. But of course the table was no longer there.

"Did he remember you?" asked my mother.

My father nodded. "Not only that, but he greeted us. He said he was glad we could come, and he asked how we knew the date of the ceremony. So that's when I told him about the new table."

"He must have liked that. It's even better than the first one."

Although my mother had spoken, he looked right at me. "I'm sorry to tell you this, son, but your father's not a very bright man. No, no—it's true. Let me tell you what happened. The provincial councillor took one look at that table, and he pulled us aside. 'Don't you see?' he asked us. And as soon as he told us the problem, we felt like such fools. And I guess I'm the biggest fool of all."

My mother was as confused as I was. "Well, what was the problem?" she finally asked, after my father had gone back to eating the soup.

My father seemed surprised that we couldn't see what he hadn't seen either before that morning. "Why," he said, "the second table was too good! If we gave that table to the temple after the provincial councillor donated the first one, do you see how bad he would look in comparison? That thought never even crossed my mind." My father was shaking his head. "I've never felt lower. The headman and I were hanging our heads, and my brother turned away completely. To think that I made them look bad along with me."

My mother and I were hanging our heads, too.

But my father said, "The provincial councillor forgave us, though. He'll arrange for another ceremony, to donate the next table. He was very understanding. He said he'll invite us personally. Of course it may be a while. They can't have two ceremonies right on top of each other."

We all sat there. I guess I was the one who finally looked over at the place where the table had been.

"Where's the second table now?" I asked.

"We took it up to the provincial councillor's office. That's fitting, you know. The wood in there inspired me to make that table in the first place."

He stood up and wandered over to his workshop, a few feet away. He picked up a piece of leftover wood and examined it, with one eye closed, so that he seemed to be winking.

I went over to him.

"What happens," he told me, "is that you spend too much time in one place, and you forget about the ways of the rest of the world."

"You don't have to worry about me. I won't spend too much time in one place."

My father put his hand on my shoulder. "Either that," he said, "or don't ever leave it at all."

He went on looking at the scraps of wood in his workshop.

FIRST THINGS WHEN?

One day, after Khun Kru Chompoo had come in the classroom and we had snapped to attention, she shook her head. "Slow. Much, much too slow."

She went out, and before she could even step back inside, we leaped up and stood at attention again.

She frowned at us. "That's a bit better. But I want you on your best behavior today. Sit!" We dropped to our seats. "Stand!" We were right back up. "Sit! Stand! Right! Left! Forward! Backward! Inhale! Exhale! Enough!"

She looked us over and said, "We'll be getting a new teacher today. And I won't have him thinking that our school is anything less than first-rate." She paused for a moment, then gave another command: "In!"

We were wondering how to follow this order when we saw someone step into the room. But we didn't dare turn our heads until Khun Kru Chompoo said, "Repeat after me: 'Good morning, Khun Kru Surasak!'"

"Good morning, Khun Kru Surasak!" we barked out.

Khun Kru Surasak was a young man in dark trousers, a clean white shirt, and a necktie. His shirt was so white that it took us a while to look all the way up to his face. He wore a belt with a gold buckle, too.

"Khun Kru Surasak has come from the college in town," said Khun Kru Chompoo. "I've already explained to him that this school's philosophy is that first things come first, and that around here, we begin at the beginning."

She stopped and squinted at us. "First things when?"

"First things first!"

She tilted her head up. "And where do we begin?"

"At the beginning!"

She turned to Khun Kru Surasak as if to say, "You see? That's how it's done."

"They're all yours," she told him. She walked across to the door and scowled at us. "I'll be back soon enough to gauge your progress," she said. Then she went out of the room.

Khun Kru Surasak bowed as she left and watched as she walked down the hall. Then he came back and stood in front of us.

Right away, he confused us by smiling.

"It's nice to meet you," he said. "I've never been to your village before, so—"

We started right in. "I've never been to your village before," we began.

He held up his hands. "No, no, no. I don't want you to repeat."

Some of us refused to be taken in. "No, no, no," we started.

Khun Kru Surasak was shaking his head. "Let me finish." We risked not repeating his words. "Thank you. What I was going to say was that I've never been to your village before, so I'd like you to tell me something about it."

We looked at him.

"Can you think of anything? What should I know?"

The girl in the front row who usually got good grades stood up.

"Is this a quiz?"

Khun Kru Surasak laughed. Somebody gasped. We had never seen a teacher laugh in the classroom before.

"It's not a quiz," he said. "Just a question."

We sat there thinking. Then the same girl stood up again. "We don't know how to answer. We've never had to talk about our village before."

"That's right," said a girl in the corner. "Everybody we know lives here already."

But then Nop, the hoarse boy who fidgeted, stood up. "I think I've got it." He fidgeted again before he tried. "The name of our village is Slippery Stream Banks Village."

We waited to see what would happen. To our surprise, Khun Kru Surasak stood beaming at Nop. "That's great!" he said.

The girl in front gave a try. "This school is called Slippery Stream Banks Village School."

"Wonderful!"

Now we were getting the hang of it. "Our temple is called Slippery Stream Banks Village Temple."

"Excellent!" said Khun Kru Surasak, who was not only smiling, but rubbing his hands together as well. "All right. Now that you've told me about your village, I'd like to know something about all of you. Who'd like to start?"

He looked around the room; finally his eyes settled on Nop. "You seem to have some ideas. Can you say something about yourself?"

Nop stood up. We noticed that he was fidgeting less than usual. Still, he was thinking hard.

"My name is Nop?" he said at last.

"Good start. But tell us more. What would you like to be when you grow up?"

We leaned forward. We were noticing more things. We noticed that Khun Kru Surasak was not staring impatiently out of the room, but he was smiling at Nop, waiting for an answer.

Nop spoke with more confidence. "I'd like to be a farmer." And then he added, "Because my father is a farmer."

Before we knew what had happened, we burst into applause. It was the first time any of us could remember that Nop had made it through a sentence in the classroom without faltering or being cut off.

Nop bowed to us and sat down. We clapped again.

The girl in front stood up next. She said, "I'd like to be a teacher—because Khun Kru Surasak is a teacher."

We didn't clap for that. The girl in front sometimes had a habit of being clever in the wrong sort of way.

Still, that got us going.

"A fisherman," said somebody. We went around the room giving answers. And I thought of mine. I wanted to be the driver for the provincial councillor.

"A singer," said someone.

"A boxer."

"A nurse."

Each of these answers was met with clapping or with laughter that meant, "No way! You're a dreamer! You're just a kid in Slippery Stream Banks Village School!"

It was almost my turn. But then Joe, the boy in front of me, stood up and said, "I'd like to be the driver for the provincial councillor!"

That got a big laugh, of course. But now I had no answer. I knew that I couldn't say the same thing as Joe. It's a sense that kids have, I guess, that one of the tricks to life is to be the first one to think of a thing.

No one would believe me or care that I had thought of Joe's answer first. I had to come up with one better.

So I stood up and said the first thing I thought of. "I want to be the provincial councillor!"

That got an even bigger laugh. And I could see why. The idea that I, a run-of-the-mill village boy, standing barefoot in a frayed, handed-down uniform, could rise beyond anything but a table maker like my father was absurd. But I liked being in the center of the laughter. It was the first time I got to enjoy the sensation of being the class clown. When I grinned, showing where two teeth were missing, everyone laughed even harder.

That's when Khun Kru Chompoo appeared in the doorway.

We stopped laughing. We stopped even faster than we had snapped to attention at the beginning of class. We stopped so fast that we could still hear the echoes of laughter as they swirled away out the windows as if they were trying to get as far from the classroom as possible.

Khun Kru Chompoo came in. I realized that I was the only one standing. I began to sit down.

"Sit!" she commanded, and two boys who were already seated stood up and sat down again.

She stood looking us over. We were aching to glance at Khun Kru Surasak, but none of us dared. Finally Khun Kru Chompoo said, "What is it? Is education so funny? Is that it? How in the world could you laugh when you knew you were here in the classroom? Here in the what?"

"In the classroom!"

She turned to Khun Kru Surasak. "I apologize for their rudeness," she said. "You're doing your best to start your career, and all they can manage is laughter."

Then she zeroed in on me. "You're at the heart of all this; I can feel it. Up!"

I stood, of course, and I fidgeted even more than Nop always did.

Khun Kru Chompoo spoke to Khun Kru Surasak. "You will develop an instinct, as I have. It comes to all teachers. But you must give it time." Then she glared back at me. "Well, Mr. Het. Could you tell me what's so funny about Khun Kru Surasak's lecture?"

I had the feeling that it was some kind of trick question, so I decided to tell her the truth. "I said that I would like to be the provincial councillor."

Nobody laughed now. And in the front of the room, Khun Kru Chompoo nodded slowly.

"The provincial councillor," she repeated. "Tell me. Was that Khun Kru Surasak's idea?"

"No, Khun Kru. It was mine."

She took a slow breath. "Listen," she said. "Don't repeat. The duties of a teacher are to give knowledge to students, to direct them toward the future, to lead them down the pathways of life." She stopped. "Lead you down what?"

"The pathways of life!"

She went on. "Let's go back to the beginning. Khun Kru Surasak is the teacher. You are the students. He speaks; you listen. He points; you look. He leads; you follow. He plants a seed, and you grow. First things first, remember. If you students try to jump ahead all the time, why have a teacher in the classroom at all?" She put her hand to her temple. "You know, you've given me another headache."

Khun Kru Chompoo took a step toward the door, then stopped. She looked back at me. "Provincial councillor?" she said. "Why don't you just take care of being a student?" She pressed both hands to her head and left the room.

We were quiet a long time before Khun Kru Surasak finally spoke. "I have to admit, I'm disappointed in you, too. I'm disappointed in your laughter."

We all hung our heads. I guess we had been hoping that he was on our side—or at least, that there were more than two sides, more than just teacher against student.

"And I'll tell you why I'm disappointed," Khun Kru Surasak went on. He was speaking calmly. "I'm disappointed that you think there's a limit to what you can do." We looked back up cautiously. "You think it's a joke to have dreams of the future. But it's no joke at all; it's your life."

Now we were looking right at him. He raised his eyebrows. "Do you know where the limit is? I'll tell you. The limit is there." And he pointed up.

We followed his finger and looked up, too.

"Now where's the limit?" he asked softly.

We sat thinking it through.

"The roof?" said someone.

"Higher," said Khun Kru Surasak.

"The top of the jackfruit tree?"

"Keep going."

The answer must have hit us together, because none of us said it.

"That's right," said Khun Kru Surasak, and we nodded.

Finally he turned back to me. "Now, can you tell us again what you'd like to be in the future?"

I stood up. I no longer felt like the class clown. "I'll tell you the truth," I said. "I never thought about being the provincial councillor before. But, if I could, it would be an honor to become our village's headman."

No one was laughing this time. We had changed a lot since the last time we laughed. Becoming headman suddenly seemed like a sensible goal. And looking around at my classmates' faces, I could see I would have lots of competition for the job.

GRENADE HANDS

The men who sat under our house at night and talked about boxing almost never agreed.

Each man had his own favorite punch, for one thing. And they argued about which part of the body was the best to take aim at. They compared feinting and jabs to the bluffs that they made in their card games—but couldn't agree on which bluffs, or which games.

Those men disagreed calmly, though. They sat back and relaxed as they argued. They knew that at the end of the night, they would get around to the one thing they could always agree on: who was the world's greatest boxer.

Of course, to them, the only world that mattered was made up of four or five villages along the Slippery Stream. Any boxer tough enough to fight his way out of that world and into one beyond it had to be pretty immortal.

Their arguments could be stopped with two words. "Grenade Hands," someone would say, and the men grew quiet. There wasn't much to disagree on once someone said that.

It doesn't take a person like me to introduce Grenade Hands. Everyone knows who he is. But not many people know that he grew up right here in Slippery Stream Banks Village.

There is a reason that nobody knows that. There is a story behind it.

I was still a baby when the story of Grenade Hands was unfolding. But I have heard that story so many times, from so many grown-ups, that I have come to believe that I took it all in myself when it happened. And I'm not the only one who believes that. Babies who are born in our village hear the story of Grenade Hands so often that they have it memorized even before they can talk.

This was at a time when the droughts were making their way to our village. That's important to the story of Grenade Hands.

Before the droughts, the pattern of life in our village was laid out before us. We'd study at Slippery Stream Banks Village School for nine years, work in the fields for a few, get married and start having children, and live out the rest of our lives with no worries.

But the droughts changed all that. Each summer, the teenagers who had finished their years at the school were sent off to struggle for work in Bangkok.

That made a gap in our village. There were the adults and the children, as there always had been. But now there were fewer and fewer people in between. And every summer, when a new group left for Bangkok, the gap got a year wider.

The adults didn't like it because they missed their children, and the children didn't like it because we liked life in our village and didn't want to leave, no matter what anyone said about money, which meant nothing to us, since we'd never had any.

That was when Grenade Hands came along. "I'm not going anywhere," he said when he grew into his teens. "I'm going to stay and bring honor to Slippery Stream Banks Village."

That was good news for the adults. Some of them, like my grandmother, were afraid that the village would soon disappear. They spent whole mornings trying to imagine life in a world without Slippery Stream Banks Village. Those people had always taken comfort in watching the next generation grow up. Now the next generation was leaving.

Grenade Hands got his nickname out back of our school. It was under the jackfruit tree. I think my uncle is right—nearly every turning point in our village's history has taken place under a tree.

That day the headman—not the same one we had a few years later when I was in the thick of growing up—put soil in a rice sack and hung it from a branch of the tree.

The headman braced himself against the rice sack and told the young boxer to come at him. "Watch this," he told the crowd that had gathered. "Wait till you see how hard this boy hits."

That made Grenade Hands a little embarrassed. His face was still red as he stepped up to the sack and led with a big roundhouse right.

Nobody knew it then, but that combination would become a Grenade Hands trademark: big right hands mixed with embarrassment at how easily he was winning.

That day under the jackfruit tree, the rope snapped just as Grenade Hands made contact. The headman flew backward. He hit the ground under the rice sack, and the rice sack split open.

A whole group rushed over to help the headman get up. After that, two things happened.

The first thing was that other men decided that they had to test Grenade Hands's punching power for themselves. For the next week it became a ritual, grown men hauling perfectly good rice sacks down to the school to sling up under the jackfruit tree and then standing behind them as the teenager came in with big roundhouse rights.

The second thing was that as soon as the rope snapped and they flew to the ground under the rice sack, they were convinced. Before they could even stand up and dust themselves off, they were volunteering to help coach Grenade Hands.

None of them had ever coached boxing, of course. But that just meant they had a lifetime of tactics saved up.

They let all of them loose on Grenade Hands.

"Bob and weave," said one man who raised chickens. "How can they hit you if you don't let 'em catch you?"

"Go for the chin," said another, whose mango orchard would die off in a drought the very next summer. "Go right up the middle. Win; chin. Got it?"

"Fake 'em out," said Uncle Song. "Make 'em think you've just about had it. Then spring your surprise."

"Wade in and slug 'em," advised Uncle Saam. "The audience will love it. Get a big following; that's what you're after."

The instinct to give advice about boxing was so strong in those men that they did not even defer to the headman, who of course had some advice of his own. "Fight like a grenade, son," he said. "Lie low for a while. Then pull out the pin and explode."

So few teenagers were around, though, that it was hard for Grenade Hands to practice. Every so often a boy from some other village would come by to spar, and as soon as the action began, the sound of the coaches took over.

"Bob!"

"Fake!"

"Wade!"

"Weave!"

"Win-chin!"

"Pull the pin!"

About the only time Grenade Hands got to be alone was when he took his training run. He woke up before dawn and ran from one end of the village to the other, out the road a ways, and then back. He skipped and ran backward and sideways, depending on which coach's house he was near at the time.

My mother told me that I used to wake up crying every morning, but as soon as Grenade Hands jogged past, I settled down and went right back to sleep.

"I must have sensed something about him," I said.

She shook her head. "All babies did that. Not only you. He had that effect on our whole village."

The headman also felt that effect. One day he went off to the city and returned with posters advertising the boxing exhibitions that were soon coming up.

"August 5. That's the big day," he told everyone. "We've registered already. This is the first step to greatness!"

Of course, as the big day came nearer, the men in the village had even more advice for Grenade Hands. They woke up early and met him as he went on his run.

"Ah, Grenade Hands," they'd say. "I was just on my way for a workout myself. And what a coincidence! I've got plenty to say about footwork!"

But since they grew tired much faster than Grenade Hands, some mornings he went through a relay team of advice-giving coaches.

"...So the thing to remember is that power comes from speed. The faster you punch, the harder your punches will feel. Well, I'm winded. But remember, the key word is speed!"

"...Good morning, Grenade Hands! Nice to see you! Did you loosen your hips? Hips are important to boxers, you know. That's where power comes from. Hips are the basis of everything. Now if you slow down just a minute, I can explain."

"Misdirection," said Uncle Song when it was his turn. "Get the other guy off guard, make him lean the wrong way, and you've got him. Not only in boxing. Misdirection is power, I tell you." Uncle Song, who was not one for jogging, waited for Grenade Hands at the end of his run and joined him in a cool-down walk.

In the final days before August 5, the whole village worked on a send-off. Ceremonies were held at the temple. Parties were thrown, with the ripest fruit and the cleanest rice put aside for Grenade Hands. Animals were caught, then released, as a way to make extra merit. People apologized for years of little misdeeds, broken promises, and white lies in order to build up our village's karma.

Meanwhile, Grenade Hands shadowboxed under the old jackfruit tree. "Eesh! Eesh!" he said as he punched.

And when the day finally came, men from our village piled onto one of those old dusty buses—except that it was a new dusty bus then. Grenade Hands climbed on the bus wearing a pair of brand-new, bright-green boxing trunks. "He looks invincible in green," everyone agreed. "Green is the color of success!"

The headman made a memorable speech that day while the bus engine idled. "Green is the color of a grenade," he said. "Let's all fight together to help pull the pin!"

Some of the men had the idea that Grenade Hands should shadowbox in the aisle of the bus on the way into town. They claimed sitting would cramp up his legs. Then another group warned him against staying in the front of the bus; it was too near the heat of the engine. But not in back with all the exhaust, either. When the bus finally left, Grenade Hands was crouched by a seat in the middle.

Right away the bus hit a bump, and Grenade Hands lurched to one side.

"That's it!" said Uncle Song. "Misdirection!"

I guess that if you want to understand the importance of that boxing exhibition, you have to remember that there was nothing that our village was known for. A group of weavers had begun to make a name for themselves at one time, but the headman's wife had not done her duties as matchmaker, and after a few marriages to outsiders, the weavers ended up two villages downstream.

Another village not far away had an abbot who had special healing powers using herbs. Farmers in a village just beyond that had hit on a new strain of rice.

Only our village had nothing to be known for, which, if you are an adult, makes it hard to go out, because eventually someone is bound to ask where you are from.

"Home of Grenade Hands!"

Now, that was an answer. And that is what the men were chanting as the bus pulled into the city. Someone even played bongoes, which came in a package deal with the bus.

Finally they pulled to a stop in front of a square white building. The headman announced, "The provincial sporting authority," and he got off the bus.

"Where's the boxing?" he asked a man who was trying to kick-start a motorcycle.

The man gave him a look.

"The boxing exhibitions," the headman went on. "We're from Slippery Stream Banks Village. We've brought the champ in to pick up his medals."

The bus gave a whoop.

But the man just said, "Uh, wait here a minute." And he went into the building.

It may have seemed odd to the headman that no other buses were around, no other chanting or bongoes. But he has never really talked about that day, and of course now he is no longer headman.

Soon a heavy bald man came out of the building and up to the bus.

"I'm the sports chief," he said. "How can I help you?"

The headman gave a startled bow and apologized for disturbing someone whose time was as valuable as the sports chief's. "We didn't expect such an honor. We just want to know the way to the boxing exhibitions."

The sports chief gave a laugh. "Exhibitions!"

"That's right. We've come all the way from Slippery Stream Banks Village."

The sports chief laughed warmly. "Is this a joke?"

"It's no joke. We may come from the countryside. But just take a look at our boxer!"

Some of the men had already laced up the gloves on Grenade Hands. They helped him to the front of the bus. He stood in the doorway, in his green trunks and gloves, and the headman said simply, "Grenade Hands."

Everyone waited for the sports chief's reaction. Would he spot the greatness in Grenade Hands immediately? Would he rush to embrace him? Would he admire the green trunks? Or would he stand quietly and ask for a demonstration, right there on the provincial sporting authority's lawn?

No, as it turned out, he would not do any of those things. He went on smiling warmly. "I asked if this is a joke," he said, "because the boxing exhibitions were held yesterday."

The headman took a step backward. The whole bus did, I've been told.

"But August 5 is today," said the headman.

"Of course it is. And the exhibitions were held August 4."

The headman looked dazed. "But the forms. The registration forms!" Someone handed them to him from the bus.

The sports chief looked them over. "Ah, I see the problem," he said. "These are the old forms. We changed the date after these forms were printed." He handed them back with a smile.

"But I got them from your office."

The sports chief nodded. "It doesn't matter where you got them. They're still the wrong forms."

"How could that be? I came here to get them myself."

"Oh, it wasn't necessary for you to come here in person." The sports chief laughed warmly. His laugh seemed to say, "The wrong day's the wrong day; what can I do about that?"

"But the boxing," the headman said. "The training. The advice!"

"Oh, don't worry too much," the sports chief said. "The exhibitions were a rousing success. I presented the medals myself! Would you like to have a look at the grounds?"

One thing that has always been true about our village. Two things, in fact. One is that we have always respected authority; the other is that we are logical thinkers. If someone as powerful as the sports chief said something, we believed it. And if he said we were wrong, then it was a fact, not a point to be argued.

No one blamed the headman that day. And certainly no one blamed the sports chief. The men on the bus just shook their heads in disappointment. "What bad luck!" they were thinking.

But the headman didn't give up. "We came all this way," he said, "and our boxer is ready. Couldn't he at least spar while he's here?"

Out came another friendly laugh from the sports chief. "I'd love to see it! But where are we going to get a partner today? Everyone fought last night, when it counted." He shook his head helplessly.

The sports chief seemed ready to lead the headman back to the bus. But the headman went on. It was his own fault, he must have reasoned, that the provincial sporting authority had changed the date of the boxing exhibitions, and now it was important for him to keep trying, on behalf of Grenade Hands, and on behalf of the busload of misinformed villagers.

"Just a workout, then. One punch! It would be a dream come true for him to throw a punch with the sports chief as a witness."

The sports chief's laugh this time seemed more of a sigh, but he said, "All right. You win. Follow me."

The men on the bus gave another whoop. They had come into town expecting a night's worth of boxing; now, after a talk with the sports chief, the promise of watching one punch had them spilling out of the bus with excitement.

"Make it an uppercut, Grenade Hands!"

"No! Your right cross!"

"Remember to throw a few feints. We're in no hurry!"

The sports chief led them to a shelter behind the white building.

"The provincial workout area number two," he announced, and they went inside.

All around the shelter were old weights and benches. But everyone was looking in the middle. Hung on a cable from the ceiling was a punching bag.

Grenade Hands started right for it.

"I'll brace it for you myself," said the sports chief.

When people have told me this story, this is the one part that they can never agree on. In a way that's good, because it seems to prove that the rest of the story is true.

Some people say that when Grenade Hands threw his big roundhouse right, the punching bag split where it hung.

Others say that the punch lifted the sports chief up off the ground, and that Grenade Hands stepped over and caught him before he could land.

Still others say that Grenade Hands missed the bag completely and caught the sports chief right on the chin; Uncle Song, who had a good angle, insists that the punch didn't go around the bag, but straight through it.

But everyone agrees that when the sports chief finally came to, the first words he spoke were, "Son, you've got a new coach."

Soon after that, Grenade Hands won a few local fights against the winners of the August 4 exhibitions; then in the regionals, he beat the big names—Iron Biceps, the Thai-ger, and the Isan Assassin. Ever since then, Grenade Hands has been, well, Grenade Hands.

"*The* Grenade Hands?" people were soon asking. He spent long hours signing autographs.

People in our village, who as you know stick to one topic at a time, talked about nothing but Grenade Hands. His success meant that everyone in the country would hear of Slippery Stream Banks Village. Soon we would be holding our heads even higher than the people from the weaving village did.

Our headman went off to see Grenade Hands's first fight in Bangkok. The headman had become a hero for getting Grenade Hands his big break, and people had donated money so that he could be there in person to hear the ring announcer say, "And, in the green corner, from Slippery Stream Banks Village, Grenade Hands!"

But our headman came back with bad news. Grenade Hands had won easily, of course; what bothered the headman was the introduction before the fight. The ring announcer had said, "And in the green corner, representing the sporting authority of Three Streams Province, Grenade Hands!"

"The provincial sporting authority?" everyone in our village said. "But that isn't fair! He is ours!"

So the headman went to talk to the sports chief again. Of course, that is why he is no longer the headman.

A man as busy as the sports chief has only so much time; he has enough to be patient with a headman who turns up for a competition on the wrong day. But it would take a rare kind of sports chief to put up with that same headman after a second mistake.

The sports chief calmly explained that he, as provincial sports chief, had done his best by claiming Grenade Hands for the whole province. Was the headman saying that the sports chief was wrong? Did the headman mean to claim Grenade Hands for his own village and deprive everyone else in the province a chance to say, "He is ours!"? Was the headman as selfish as that?

The headman was so ashamed that he not only resigned as headman, but he went on to take a job in the sports chief's office, where he could learn more about unselfish behavior. Every now and then some of the men from our village went to town to watch a fight on TV; when they gathered at our house later on, they talked about seeing the ex-headman in the background when the sports chief was introduced before the fight as Grenade Hands's manager, coach, and founder.

Under our house, the men worked their way back through the story of Grenade Hands until they reached the beginning, under the jackfruit tree. And then the disagreements started up once again.

"The beginning is the best part of the story. He should have left it at that."

"No, no. Those punches wouldn't mean anything if he hadn't gone on to greatness."

"How much greatness does he need? He was right to go on. But he should've just fought locally to bring credit to the village, where it matters."

"Nobody can blame him for how far he went. Besides, who cares if the world doesn't know where he comes from? As long as we know ourselves, that's what counts."

And that's how it went until the men drifted off into the night.

YOU LOSE SOME

Even we had to admit that nothing much ever happened in our village. One day was the same as the next. So when some little event did come along, like when Nop, the fidgety boy, slipped into the cesspool at the temple, not only did everyone go running to look, but it was all people talked about for weeks.

As days passed and no new event came along, the stories about Nop grew and grew. The first stories said that the cement cover had cracked when he stepped on it. Then word came that he had been pushed in by accident. Soon new stories grew about who did the pushing, and why.

And when nothing else happened, we were forced to keep talking about Nop. He had jumped into the cesspool on an order from a ghost. No, that wasn't it—he had done it because of an old superstition. No again—he had jumped in on a dare, in order to win a lifetime supply of fermented fish sauce for his mother.

All that was too bad if you happened to be Nop. His bad luck—and all the gossip that followed—taught us that we'd better be doubly careful ourselves.

Eventually, the stories died down, and the days went back to being the same. Our village was in a slow period like that, between stories, when Khun Kru Surasak came to our school.

A new teacher, with new methods, was big news in our village, where almost everyone had been taught by Khun Kru Chompoo. Stories about Khun Kru Surasak traveled fast. They traveled out through the village and boomeranged back to the school.

He's single! His father sells radios! He lives on the second-widest street in the city!

Khun Kru Surasak laughed when he heard the stories going around about himself. "I've never been interesting to anyone before," he said. "Maybe we should give the village some real things to talk about."

Sometimes it seemed that he was making fun of us for having such a slow pace to our lives. He came in every morning and asked, "What's new?" knowing the answer full well.

"Nothing," we told him.

"Nothing?" he asked. "Not a thing?"

"Nothing," we told him again.

At first he just sighed and got on with teaching. But his sighs were growing longer each day. Finally, he said, "I've had it with 'nothing.' I never want to hear 'nothing' again. Understand?"

We looked at him blankly.

"I want all of you to go out of this room, and don't come back until you've found something about this school that you never noticed before. Something new. Ready? Go!"

We gave a shout and sprinted away, fanning out over the schoolyard. Then we gave individual shouts as we made our discoveries, most of us in no time at all. And even though we could have stayed out of the classroom much longer, we sprinted back to report on what we had found.

"I found a new anthill under the jackfruit tree," someone said.

"The jasmine bush has a new set of buds."

"There's a new dog hanging around the boys' bathroom."

"Aw, he was there last week."

"Well, I never saw him before."

Khun Kru Surasak was about to teach us that the important thing was that we had used the word *new*, when just then Nop returned to the classroom. He was the last to come back.

"I found a new box," Nop said. "Full of paper and colored pencils."

"Ah," said Khun Kru Surasak. "You discovered my secret."

That's when he announced we were having an art contest. He told us to draw anything in the village we wanted to. The teachers would decide on a winner. He handed out paper, and our eyes grew big when he gave us each a small set of colored pencils.

"Donated by the Red Cat Supply Store in town," he told us. "I promised I'd mention their name."

I spent the weekend drawing pictures. I drew one of a staircase that led up to nothing. I drew one of my father at work on a table and another of my mother cooking soup. I drew my sister doing her homework under our mango tree, and I would have drawn more, but I ran out of Red Cat supplies.

Khun Kru Surasak was right about one thing. Whenever I tried to draw anything, I discovered new details about it—even about my father, whose face I had seen every day of my life. And yet, drawing his picture, I discovered what a small forehead he had. His hairline came down almost right to his eyebrows. What a thing not to have noticed!

Of course, after that day I noticed people's hairlines, sometimes more than I noticed their eyes. Cheeks, too, I noticed, and nostrils.

I noticed these things because I was trying to draw pictures. I had no idea I was developing a "style."

I took my drawings to school and waited to hear Khun Kru Surasak's praise.

"What's new?" he asked us that morning, and we all had stories to tell. I talked about my father's hairline. The girl in front had learned that her family's house was built on a slant. Nop told about the new cement cover that had been put on the cesspool, which he had drawn from the point of view of a bird, looking down for new things in the village that he could go home to his nest and talk about with his family.

"Want to see that picture?" Nop asked us.

We were all breathing in to shout, "Yes!" when Khun Kru Surasak held up his hands.

"Not yet," he said. No one was more disappointed than I was when he just collected the drawings and put them all in a box.

But we forgot about them a moment later when he said, "It's time to announce a new contest."

We sat forward. Contests were becoming Khun Kru Surasak's trademark, taking the place of Khun Kru Chompoo's famous quizzes.

"Next Friday," he said, "will be Sports Day. We'll divide into teams, and each team will have a color. There will be all kinds of races. We will cheer and compete."

We let out a whoop. We chose our teams and events, and we spent every day practicing.

I was Sky Blue. And as Sports Day came nearer, I noticed that I was spending more and more time with other Sky Bluers and less with kids from other colors. We invented a password and cheered one another in class. We competed to raise our hands first and give the right answer.

"The answer is five!"

"That's right!"

"Go, Sky Blue!"

But nothing prepared us for what happened on the morning of Sports Day, before the games even started. As we were lined up in front of the school, finishing the national anthem, the old black grocery supply truck pulled up, and Khun Kru Surasak went out to meet it.

"Just in time," he told the driver as they unloaded boxes. Then he turned to us. "OK, everyone. Come get your T-shirts!"

I don't know when I've felt more excited than I did as I was handed my shirt. Remember, we were kids who had almost nothing. We got our clothes secondhand from brothers or sisters or cousins. Even if our mothers bought things from a supply truck that passed through the village, those clothes weren't new, either. They fit, though, and that's all we could imagine expecting. Our collars were frayed; our white shirts always had a gray tint.

But these T-shirts were brand-new, still wrapped in plastic. They were bright—even shiny—in the colors of each of the teams. We put them on. They were almost blinding against the background of our brown wooden school, with the gray dusty soil around it.

That must have been something to see. I bet if we had looked at the sky that day, we would have seen birds up there, looking down enjoying the view.

"These shirts have been paid for by sponsors in town," said Khun Kru Surasak. "Next week, you'll write thank-you letters. But now, let's play sports!"

All that day we ran around in shirts bearing the names of businesses we'd never heard of. They were in bold letters on the back of each shirt. There were Three Friends Bakery and Aunt Oom's Soup Shop. I had the Love Arrow Nightclub.

We had a lot of contests that year with Khun Kru Surasak—a singing contest, I remember, and a spelling bee—but those shirts were the highlight. We wore them as often as we could, as fast as our mothers could wash them. You could see them around our village for years after that, long after the results of the games were forgotten, long after the names of the sponsors had worn off.

Sports Day was what our village talked about now. Everyone came to watch, and a shelter was set up, with armchairs for Khun Kru Chompoo and the headman.

My race was the one-lap run.

That was once around the soccer field. A game was going on in the middle, Green against Yellow, raising a big cloud of dust. Our group of all different colors ran around the outside.

Just before our race began, Uncle Song came up to me from out of the crowd. "It's a long way around the field," he said. "Those other guys will burn themselves out. You hang back. Save your strength. When they get tired, you run past them and win." He winked at me. "Always have a strategy, Het. That's the secret. I used to be a runner myself, you know."

Eight of us ran. The headman was the starter. Khun Kru Surasak's father had donated a microphone and speakers, and the headman's words boomed much louder than necessary out across the ricefields. "Mark. Set. Go!"

Everyone shouted. The rest of the runners took off at top speed, without any sign of a strategy. I hung back. They went past the first goal, and I was dead last. I was confident, though. I was the most confident boy in the race.

We ran past my group of teammates, Sky Blue, in the crowd. "What's with you, Het?" they shouted. "The race started already, you know. Get moving!" I smiled and gave them thumbs up.

I let the other runners widen their lead. We ran down the far side, with me trailing, and one voice boomed out over the others.

"I'm betting on you, Het!" shouted Uncle Song.

It's funny, but just when I heard him, I felt my confidence slip. "How long till they burn themselves out?" I was thinking. "How far behind should I let myself get?"

As they passed the far goal, they were running faster than ever, powered on by the crowd and by their bright shirts. I hadn't counted on that. I ran harder now myself.

But it was too late. Those other guys ran in a clump at full speed the whole way around the field, and when they came down the backstretch, they spread out in a line, running their fastest. Seven brightly colored shirts racing through the dust, like a rainbow. It was something to see, all right, and I saw it all—from behind. The other runners crossed the line together. A seven-way tie! Then they doubled over with their hands on their knees, panting.

I came in last. I had saved my strength, and when I crossed the line, I wasn't even tired. I could have run a whole extra lap. I was standing up straight, barely breathing, watching the other guys gasp.

I was turning away when someone put a hand on my shoulder.

"Let's talk for a minute," said Khun Kru Surasak.

He led me away from the crowd. I thought sure he would tell me how disappointed he was in my running. The closer he led me to the school building, the surer I became.

In our village, we had never learned to be upset about losing. "You win some, you lose some," we had been taught. But I was afraid that Khun Kru Surasak had seen that I hadn't done my best. I walked with my head down, behind him.

He took me to the room with my father's table and sat on one of the rickety chairs.

"You like competing, don't you?" he said.

"Everyone does."

He nodded. "How do you feel about not coming in first?"

I hung my head. "My strategy backfired. I'm sorry. Next time, I'll go faster."

Khun Kru Surasak gave a laugh. "I wasn't talking about running," he said. "I was talking about art!" He pointed to some papers on the table. I realized that they were my drawings.

"Your pictures are good," he said. "You've got a talent for drawing. Did anyone ever tell you that before?"

"Nobody ever told me I had a talent for anything."

"It's true." He picked up the pictures. "You've got a real knack for hairlines," he said. "And just look at these nostrils!" He was shaking his head as he went through the drawings. His own hairline was a little bit jagged.

He looked back at me. "I wanted to tell you how much I liked these. I don't want you to feel bad when you find out you didn't win the contest."

I had enjoyed drawing so much that I had forgotten there would be a winner at all. But I said, "I didn't?"

Khun Kru Surasak shook his head. "I was outvoted. I'm just a rookie teacher, remember. That's one of the ways of the world."

I guess I still looked confused, because he said, "Are you interested in being an artist?"

"Sure. I like drawing. I like noticing things."

"Good." He handed me another box of colored pencils, much brighter than the first set we'd all gotten. "These weren't donated. I bought them for you myself. I want you to practice. Take these and keep drawing."

I had to force myself to look up from them. "Thank you," I said. "I will. I'll draw everything I can think of."

He laughed again. "Well, I'm ready to help you. I've done some drawing myself, you know." He stood up. "Now we'd better get back to the sports."

We got back to the crowd just as the soccer game ended. Khun Kru Surasak took the microphone.

"The soccer game is over," he announced. "Congratulations to Green!" The Green team gave a big cheer. "And to Yellow, who also played well." A smaller cheer came.

"And now it's time for a special award. It's an honor to ask Khun Kru Chompoo to announce the winner of the first Slippery Stream Banks Village School art contest!"

There was some clapping. It's hard to make a sports crowd get worked up over art. Still, the quiet meant that everyone was listening.

"We had so many good drawings, it was hard to choose," said Khun Kru Surasak. "But at last we selected a winner. And the winner is…" With a bow, he handed the microphone to Khun Kru Chompoo.

"The winner is…Noppadol Tiso!" That was Nop! He ran out from his group of Yellow teammates and accepted his prize from Khun Kru Chompoo: more drawing paper and another set of Red Cat Supply pencils. Khun Kru Surasak held up the winning picture, of a bird looking down at Nop in the cesspool.

But Nop was no longer the boy who had been in the cesspool; now he was the art contest winner. He ran back to his teammates, who gave a big cheer and mobbed him.

The crowd cheered now, too; I might have cheered loudest of all.

Then came the next soccer game, between Sky Blue and Pink.

As I went out on the field, I had a strange feeling. "Be careful," I said to myself. "You're an artist now, not an athlete."

Yet as I ran down the field, raising dust, I felt I was running faster than ever, much faster than the boys who had just beaten me in the one-lap run. When the ball came to me, I dribbled it once and kicked harder than I ever had before.

"You're an athlete now, not an artist," I told myself, and then *wham*!

Like that, I was no longer the boy who had lost the one-lap run. Now I was the boy who had taken a gigantic kick and missed the ball completely in front of every pair of eyes in the village. I gave a shout in mid-air, probably just like the shout that Nop gave when he fell into the cesspool. I landed flat on the Love Arrow Nightclub.

That raised the biggest dust cloud of Sports Day. It drew a cheer from the crowd, and it brought the Sky Blue and Pink teams together in deep, joyous laughter.

Even the birds laughed at that one. I know they did, because Nop drew a picture of them with his new Red Cat pencils, and he gave it to me the next day.

DROUGHT

The droughts began a few years before I was born and became a regular feature of life in our village. Some lasted for months at a time. Then the rains finally came, and after that a new drought started in.

But at least the droughts gave us something to talk about. Nobody had more stories than my grandmother, who had been living there so long that she could remember when there were no droughts at all. To me, droughts were common and expected; to her, they were still a new part of life.

"One evening in May," she told me, "when the rainy season was supposed to get started, your father and I were out by the edge of the ricefields, and it didn't rain. He looked at the sky and said, 'Hmm.'

"A week or so later as we were out by those very same ricefields, it still wasn't raining. 'Hmm,' your father said again."

My grandmother let the significance of the story sink in. Then, to be sure, she explained.

"Anybody can feel the first drops at the start of a rainstorm. But how many people notice the start of a drought? Your father knew from the very first moments that the droughts would take over our village."

My father, who was too good a son to disagree with his mother directly, shook his head slowly. "Are you sure that's exactly what happened?"

My grandmother ignored him. "How many people know that the first extra ache is the start of old age? Well, your father knew. That's what he meant with his *hmm*. He meant, 'Here comes a decade of suffering.'"

She leaned toward me. "When you live in a place where nothing new ever comes, you learn to wait for the old things to come back. Your father was looking forward to the return of the rainy season. But he knew right away it wouldn't come."

That night some of the villagers came to our house to discuss the latest drought.

"The Slippery Stream is down two inches," said one of them.

"How do you know?"

"I made a mark on a tree last year, and now the water's below it."

"Well, how do you know the tree didn't grow?"

"Hmm."

I watched as everyone sat chewing sunflower seeds. I was learning that it took meetings like this to solve the world's many problems.

"We can't let it drag on," said Nop's father.

"We'll have to take action."

"Action," the others agreed, nodding and chewing with new energy. "Like what?"

Uncle Saam was the first to speak up. "Rationing water. Remember, we did that the last time."

"I remember," said a woman whose papaya trees wound up surviving the drought. "Three scoops per bath for adults, two scoops for children under twelve."

"All right. Rationing. What else?"

The group thought again.

"Educate the kids. Teach them the value of conservation."

"Good. And let's push for reforestation."

"How about holding an extra bamboo-rocket festival?"

"That's worth a try. Any other ideas?"

My father began nodding. "Hmm," he said.

The others turned toward him. It wasn't often that my father spoke at these meetings. He usually just listened, which is one reason most people liked him.

"What about a sacrifice?" he said.

The papaya woman nodded. "You mean sacrifice a thing, right? Like the old bridge."

Even I had heard about the old footbridge. It used to sag low over the Slippery Stream. The village had decided that a low-hanging bridge was bad luck. The skies were afraid to rain because the stream might flood and wash out the bridge. The village built a new footbridge that arched up over the stream instead.

Of course, that did not bring more rain. Still, I loved hearing stories like that. It made me feel important, living in a place where decisions had been made back before I was born.

But my father was shaking his head. "Not quite like the bridge," he said. "My idea is to sacrifice water. Give up a little to get a whole lot more back."

One thing about our village: we were willing to give new things a try. Or maybe it was the threat of more droughts that made us so open-minded. People were nodding, trying to make it make sense.

"How much water?" they asked. "Give it up how?" They looked at my father.

"I haven't thought it all the way through. But we all know that if we want to get something, we have to give something up first. That's one of the main facts of life."

That made sense to the group. "We'll add that to the list," they said. They wrote their ideas down. Rationing. Reforestation. Education. Bamboo-rocket festival. Water sacrifice.

"We'll take this to the headman in the morning," they said. "He's sure to have more ideas of his own."

But at that moment the headman appeared, walking in toward our house from the lane. I always watched him carefully, wondering if I had the makings of a headman myself.

"I have some good news," he said. "I thought I'd let you talk things over before I broke it to you. I just heard today that a government minister will come to our village next week to check on the effects of the drought."

"A minister!"

"Well, perhaps not the minister himself," said the headman. "It will be an assistant to one of his staff."

For the next week, no one talked about anything else. We got busy planning for the big day. Some people wanted to lay out a tour of the village so that the assistant to the minister's staff would be sure to see the dustiest places. Others thought we should do just the opposite: water a few places down, then take the assistant there. That way he would see how hard we were working to battle the drought.

One night, people from all over the village were making a list of points that the headman should bring up in his meeting with the assistant. They mentioned the withered rice seedlings, the weak chickens, and the dry cracks that spread out through the soil. I sat to the side and made a list of my own.

1. Dust on the leaves. Not only were leaves of the weeds and old plants in our village browner than usual, but layers of dust kept settling on them, making them look even drier. No rain came to wash the leaves off.

2. Fewer frogs. This should have been the time of year when the frogs gathered to sing out to one another after rainstorms. But with no storms, we had hardly any frogs, not even in the bathroom at night. And the few frogs we did see looked bored.

3. Dust on the frogs. They had nowhere to go to wash off. There was dust on the buffaloes, too.

One thing that I didn't write down was how cheerful everyone stayed during the drought. We weren't complainers. We figured that we must have done something wrong somewhere along the line, and the drought was the price we were paying. "We deserve this, we guess," was our attitude.

And we felt we deserved the good things that came along, too, like the visit from the assistant to the minister's staff. Surely he would size up our problems and solve them. We believed that whatever good deeds our village might have done were finally improving our luck.

Besides, there was a bonus for us kids. The assistant would come in a helicopter. We cheered when we heard that. We had never seen one before. Khun Kru Chompoo, in her last few months on the job, spent the whole week training us for the helicopter's arrival, teaching us to stand in straight lines at attention.

"The reputation of the entire Slippery Stream region is at stake," she said. "Ten-hut!"

All over the village, people were busy preparing. Men made practice runs of the tour route, stopping to gesture and bow. Women planned a menu for the assistant and the helicopter pilot, cooking snacks for them to take along home. The headman himself could be seen walking the ricefields, where he practiced giving meaningful nods.

On the big day, two trucks full of soldiers and police officers arrived and stood guard at the soccer field, where the helicopter was scheduled to land. Everyone in our village stood waiting. Finally we heard the helicopter approaching.

"Ten-hut!" said Khun Kru Chompoo.

The helicopter came toward us surprisingly fast as it flew over Slippery Stream Bed Village. We felt proud as we thought of those villagers, watching the helicopter fly over their heads, right toward us.

But since no helicopter had ever flown to Slippery Stream Banks Village before, we weren't prepared for what happened. The helicopter flew in over the soccer field and began its descent. Our eyes and mouths were wide open. But as the helicopter came lower, with its big blades chopping, we were reminded of why it was here. The wind from the blades blew the dust off the ground, into our faces.

We closed our eyes, and we had to turn away. And then, just like that, the helicopter rose back into the air.

"He's leaving!" we thought. "He was so offended when we turned our backs that he changed his mind!"

But the helicopter was hovering high up over our heads. One of the soldiers ran to the headman.

"They can't land with all this dust!" he shouted.

The headman came over to us. "Boys. Go grab some buckets from the supply closet and bring water from the storage tank as fast as you can. Go!"

We sprinted away for the buckets. The storage tank stood next to the school building. It collected rain from the roof during the rainy season, and we used that water throughout the rest of the year. Now here we were running with bucket after bucket of the water, which the soldiers poured out on the soccer field. Then we ran back for more.

We ran two boys to a bucket. Some of the water sloshed out as we carried it, making a trail between the school and the field. Slowly, though, a wet patch spread out. And just as the storage tank went dry, the helicopter descended again.

Dust still blew toward us, but much less this time. We were able to face forward as the helicopter touched down at midfield. A group of soldiers rushed over to let out the assistant to the minister's staff.

He was dressed in a dark suit. Another man held an umbrella out over his head as he walked toward us. He came right down the trail made by the water that had sloshed from the buckets.

The headman stepped forward to greet him, and the assistant cleared his throat. We all leaned forward to listen.

"Good afternoon, friends," he began. He stopped for a moment, and we clapped. "I'm here on behalf of the minister of the public good. I want to remind you that the minister is keeping abreast of your situation, and we assure you that we know how you feel."

We clapped again, just as Khun Kru Chompoo had taught us.

"Unfortunately, I'm on a tight schedule today, and our landing here took so long that I won't have time for the inspection tour we had planned. I am sorry about that. But I do have with me a package of suggestions authorized by the minister himself, designed specifically for your village."

The man with the umbrella took out a black folder and bowed. The assistant snapped the black folder open.

"The first step," he read, "is rationing of water." He stopped as if he were waiting for more clapping. When it didn't come, he went on. "The next step is reforestation. More trees mean more rainfall. And as you might expect, the minister stands ready with low-interest loans to pay for new saplings."

He paused again. We no longer clapped, and that seemed to throw off his timing. He cleared his throat and went on.

"The third step that the minister wishes to emphasize is education. Teach our children the importance of water conservation. That is precisely the reason we touched down on school grounds today."

He snapped the folder shut. "The minister urges you to follow these steps strictly in your quest for a damper tomorrow." He smiled. "And I myself have one more suggestion that I'm sure will pay dividends. I know that in this region you hold bamboo-rocket festivals each year to ask the sky to provide rain. Well, why not hold a bonus festival this year? My point is, what could it hurt?"

He gave us his biggest smile yet. "I'm running late for my next appointment. But I won't forget your warm welcome here today, and I'll file a full report with the minister as soon as we return to the office. Goodbye to all of you fine people!"

The assistant turned toward the helicopter. But while he was speaking, the sun and the blades had dried up the water we'd poured, and the dust was getting thicker again. It blew hard into his face. He had to turn and walk to the helicopter backward. We shielded our eyes and watched the soldiers rush over to steer him.

That night the group gathered at our house, as usual. But this time the feeling was different. Everyone stared at the ground or out at the darkness. It was the quietest I could remember our village. No one even bothered to chew any sunflower seeds.

Nop's father was holding the list of suggestions they had written.

"Better save that," someone said. "That qualifies you to be the minister of the public good."

"It's not the list," someone else said. "It's the folder you carry it in. That is the real qualification." People shook their heads and were quiet again.

The headman arrived, and for a few moments he stood there, too tired to say anything. Finally he sighed, and he opened his mouth to speak.

Instead of his voice, we heard an odd sound.

We all looked up. "What was that?"

"The helicopter," Nop's father said. "The assistant to the minister's staff must be coming back."

"That's not a helicopter. That's—"

The sound came again.

"That's thunder!" said my mother.

We all jumped up and looked off at the sky. Sure enough, between branches of the mango tree, we saw lightning.

We stood there cheering. Shouts came from all over the village. Then we listened to the low rumble, still far away.

"How far off is it?" we were asking. "Is it coming this way?" We grew quiet again, trying to size up the thunder.

It was Uncle Song who began chuckling. He nodded at first; then he was shaking his head.

"Genius," he said slowly. "That man is a genius."

The rest of us looked at him. "What's that? Who?"

Uncle Song seemed surprised. "Why, the assistant to the minister's staff. Sheer genius."

"A genius? How do you figure?"

"Don't you see?" He turned to the headman. "You see it, don't you? Don't you see what he did?"

The headman coughed. "Maybe you'd better explain."

Uncle Song sat smiling and shaking his head. "The sacrifice."

"How do you mean?"

"The water sacrifice! Don't you remember? We poured all that water today."

Everyone squinted at him.

But the headman was nodding. "You're right," he said slowly. "I get it now. We poured all that water out on the field. That was the sacrifice."

People made grunts of understanding. "You think he had that planned?"

The headman answered again. "Of course it was a plan. I see everything now. Why, he didn't have to speak to us at all! As soon as he got us to pour out that water, his job was done!"

Now the rest nodded. "It makes sense," they were saying. "I'll admit it; I was thinking it was a waste to pour all that good water. He sure had me fooled."

"He had all of us fooled. That's why he works for the ministry, and we don't!"

"He didn't take any credit, either. He never even mentioned the sacrifice."

"It's like he tricked us for our own good."

"That's genius, all right."

For a long time they stood talking. They broke out their sunflower seeds, too.

After a while the headman asked for some quiet. "Let's see what's happening with our storm."

We stared into the darkness, out through the branches of the mango tree. Our village had grown louder now, though, so the thunder was harder to hear. And we couldn't quite find the place in the sky where we had just seen the lightning.

Finally we heard a low rumble. "Aha!" said someone. But the rumble hadn't come from the sky; it came from right there, under the house.

The rumble was coming again.

It was my father. "Hmm," he was saying. "Hmm."

One by one, we joined in.

DUST IN OUR VEINS

All this time I was still drawing pictures.

My favorite thing to draw was the house where I would live in the future.

My father had shown me the place many times. He called it "The Site." It was in back of our house, on the way through the Bamboo Garden to the ricefields.

"Right here," my father said. "We'll build it at an angle, like this." He walked me through it. "Back here's the kitchen. We can dig the septic tanks there." He said that someday I would have a wife and children of my own. "That's the way life works," he told me.

The house I kept drawing looked like a big box on stilts. A stairway led up from the ground, and I drew square windows.

"Add details," Khun Kru Surasak told me in art class. "That's what gets pictures noticed. Here. Look at this picture Nop's drawing."

Nop's pictures were packed full of details. His imagination swirled all around as he drew. Khun Kru Surasak sometimes said, "Look, Nop, you've got some white space left in the corner," and Nop bent down and filled the space with a wide-eyed bird, looking on, or maybe a jackfruit rolling into the picture.

I wasn't like that. My drawing was clearer than Nop's, but I left empty space all around. I drew what I saw and then stopped.

"That's a nice house," Khun Kru Surasak told me. "And I like all those bamboo tables. But where are the people? Does anything happen around there?"

We held those art classes after school on Tuesdays and Thursdays. I wanted to go every day, but Khun Kru Surasak wouldn't allow it.

"Great artists divide their lives in two parts," he said. "Only one part is for drawing. The other part is for observing, for finding new things to draw."

He had a drawing textbook that he sometimes read to us. "'Contrasts,'" he read. "'Contrasts make your work come alive. Large things and small. Moisture and dust. Cement walls in contrast with nature.'" Khun Kru Surasak looked up from the book. "Now there are some contrasts for you, boys."

I sat, nodding and taking it all in. But Nop kept on drawing. When Khun Kru Surasak stopped and repeated the word *contrasts*, Nop just bent lower over his paper and pressed down harder on his Red Cat pencil.

I showed the pictures I drew to my parents. "That's your house, all right," my father said. "It's just like I described it to you." He took a long time over the pictures, chuckling in admiration. He went back to The Site and held them up. He was imagining the future.

But not all my pictures were of houses. "Here's a picture of a kitchen," said my mother one time, in surprise.

"That's our kitchen," I told her.

"So it is. What's this thing down here in the corner?"

"That's a mango."

My mother examined it closely.

"Why is it bigger than the rice sack?"

"Contrast," I said.

My father kept all my pictures and showed them to the neighbors when they came to sit under the house and talk. "Look at this house. That's exactly the way we're going to build it, over there behind that bamboo." Or, "Take a look at this one. What do you think that is down there in the corner? Come on, take a good look!"

Those pictures brought out a talkative side that I'd never before seen in my father. They brought out the differences between Nop and me, too.

Some days in class, Nop filled three or four sheets full of birds' eyes and jackfruits and haystacks, while I spent that same time trying to get the roof of one house just right.

"Don't you want a bird perching up there?" asked Khun Kru Surasak. "How about a jackfruit tree growing beside it? That would be a nice contrast."

To Nop he said, "Your imagination is going great guns! Sit back and rest for a minute." To me he said, "Het, let yourself go. You are too young to become a perfectionist."

Most days I came home with only one drawing. "I'm sorry," I said to my parents. "I'm afraid I'm becoming a perfectionist."

I was sure my father would be disappointed. But he put his arm around me, beaming.

"You get that from me," he said proudly. "Every table I make, it has to be perfect. And not only does it have to be perfect, but the next one has to be even better." He patted me on the shoulder. "Now let's go have a look at The Site."

One day after art class, Khun Kru Surasak was talking to Nop and me as we came out of school. "You boys are lucky. Some people go their whole lives without ever finding a thing that they're good at. You're barely twelve years old, and already you're becoming real artists." We turned down the lane of our village. "But you need to keep learning. There are whole worlds out there you've never even thought of. There's more to life than bamboo and jackfruit." He spread out his arms toward the world. "Keep working, you two. Art can take you away from all this." He gave a laugh as he went off to the room where he lived in back of the grocery.

At home I told my parents what Khun Kru Surasak had said.

My mother was pounding chilies for dinner. "He said that? Khun Kru Surasak said, 'Art can take you away from all this'?"

"That's what he said. But I don't understand. What does he mean by 'all this'?"

My father had been chewing sunflower seeds, but now he just let them wait. "What I don't understand," he said, "is what he means by 'take you away.'"

My father was still sitting there later when the neighbors drifted in and sat down. He told them the story. "What does he mean, 'take you away'? What does he mean by that?"

Uncle Saam was shaking his head. "What is all this about 'art,' anyway? What can art do?"

"Art never grew any rice," said a farmer.

"Or kept the rain off our heads in a storm," said a woman who sewed patches on clothes.

They sat talking and helping themselves to sunflower seeds.

The next Tuesday morning as I was leaving for school, my father, who was squatting down snapping twigs, spoke up.

"Come straight home from school, Het. I need you to help gather coconuts."

"I have art class today," I reminded him.

"It will be too dark after that. Take a day off from art."

When I told Khun Kru Surasak, he said, "Well, co-conuts are coconuts. You'd better go help your father."

Then Nop came and said that his father wanted him to help clear branches from a tree that had been cut down that morning.

"All right, then," said Khun Kru Surasak. "I'll see you on Thursday."

But on Thursday afternoon our fathers were wait-ing in front of the school.

"Hurry up, Nop," said Nop's father. "One of the chickens is sick." They walked off in the heat.

My father put his hand on my shoulder. "The fish are gigantic today. I wouldn't want you to miss out. Let's get down to The Place."

I took a step along with my father, then turned back to Khun Kru Surasak.

"I'm sorry," I told him.

He shook his head. "That's all right. You go ahead. Next week you can draw pictures of gigantic fish." As he turned back toward the school, his shoulders seemed to be sagging.

"Khun Kru Surasak," I said, and he stopped. "Would you like to go fishing with us?"

Khun Kru Surasak turned and looked at my father. "Is it all right with you?"

My father, who was wearing his big rubber boots, squinted off in the direction of the stream. "It doesn't matter what I think. Everything's up to the fish."

He led the way to The Place and in no time at all had caught three good-sized fish.

"They're not quite gigantic," he apologized as he shook out his net.

"They're big enough for my mouth," I said, making our village's traditional joke.

My father turned to Khun Kru Surasak. "Around here, there's only one thing to do after you invite someone to catch fish with you. And that's to invite him to eat with you, too."

Soon a crowd had gathered at our house, and my uncles broke out a bucket of rice wine. At parties in our village, everyone shared the same glass. Each person dipped it in the bucket, had a drink, and then passed it on.

"The first glass goes to Khun Kru Surasak!"

Cheers went up, and the glass made its way around the circle.

Then my mother brought out the grilled fish.

"Khun Kru Surasak, help yourself first!"

There was roast coconut, too.

"Send this around to our most special guest!"

More cheers went up when Khun Kru Surasak took seconds, and again when he drank the next glass of wine.

"Khun Kru Surasak! Sing a song!"

"Khun Kru Surasak! Tell a joke!"

"Khun Kru Surasak! Tell us how you feel about Slippery Stream Banks Village!"

For the first time, there was quiet. Everyone waited for Khun Kru Surasak to speak. He smiled, and the rice wine shone in his eyes.

"You know," he said. "Right now I'm thinking of the staircase that leads up to nothing. The staircase stops in midair."

Everyone was looking at Khun Kru Surasak.

"That's how I felt about Slippery Stream Banks Village before tonight. I felt I had climbed the staircase already, but I didn't know where to step next. There was no second floor. But tonight, I've found it. And I'm glad to say that all of you are my second floor. Thank you." There was more silence for a moment until he added, "That's all." Then a new cheer went up. Khun Kru Surasak chewed on a piece of roast coconut.

Before long he stood up to go.

"Another glass, Khun Kru Surasak!"

"The party's not over!"

"There's still more rice wine!"

But Khun Kru Surasak smiled and said thank you, then made his way down the lane.

For a long time everyone sat in silence. Some rice wine was still left in the bucket.

"Well, what do you think?"

Slowly people cleared their throats.

"I think," someone said, "it would take a lot of rainy seasons to wash the city off him."

"It would. And a lot of rice wine to wash it out."

"He hardly even touched it."

"Well, it's wet enough for my mouth. Who's hiding that glass, anyway?"

My parents came over to my sister and me as the drinking resumed. "Bedtime," they said, and we went upstairs.

Before I could fall asleep, my mother came and knelt beside my mosquito net. "I don't know if you should have heard that, Het. He's your teacher, after all."

"I'm all right."

My mother looked down at me. Moonlight came in through the window.

"Good," she said. "Now get some sleep." She went back downstairs.

I lay on my mat listening to the toasts being drunk outside. I could hear the dip of the glass in the bucket.

"Here's to Slippery Stream Banks Village!"

"Here's to the cracks in the ricefields!"

"Here's to the dust in our veins!"

I went over and sat by the window. A few sheets of paper lay on one of my father's perfect tables. There was just enough light for me to start sketching while the party went on down below.

SKINNY LIZARDS

One afternoon my uncles were sitting under our house, talking about the time our village finally got electricity.

After one story, I sat laughing. "I remember that," I said.

"Impossible!" they told me. "You weren't even born then."

"I was so. I remember everything about it."

"Are you sure about that? It might just be that you've heard these stories so many times, you think you were there."

At that moment two men passed on their way down the lane, and my uncles called them in. "Refresh our memories," my uncles said. "When did we first get electricity?"

The two men stood scratching their heads. One began counting on his fingers; the other looked back at the lane, as if he was picturing events in his mind.

"It seems to me it was just about two or three years ago," the second one said.

"Aw, go on," said the first man. He turned to my uncles. "The problem with him is, he's told those electricity stories so many times, they're still as fresh in his mind as things that happened last week."

The second man nodded. "Fresher," he agreed.

The two men went off, still counting and looking here and there at the lane.

"That's the thing about our village," said Uncle Saam as he watched them go. "Nobody's ever written down our history."

Uncle Song was shaking his head. "It isn't that. Everybody can tell you exactly what happened. The problem is that no one can tell you when."

"You may be right."

"Let's check." Uncle Song turned to me. "Tell me, Het. What used to be out behind the temple?"

"You mean where the dried-up old swamp is now?"

"That's right."

"Well, it used to be the old swamp!"

"Exactly." Uncle Song gave a sly look and leaned forward. "Now, when did the old swamp dry up?"

"I don't know," I said finally.

"There. You see? And the thing of it is, I don't know either!" He sat back. "How long has it been since the stream overflowed? When did we put down the new planks on the footbridge? In what year did I build my pigsty? When did I tear it back down?"

Uncle Saam was nodding. "I see what you mean. I don't know when any of those things happened. Yet I can see them all clearly."

Uncle Song patted my shoulder. "So, Het, that shows you how fouled-up someone's memory can get."

"But it doesn't mean I can't remember the electricity!"

My uncles exchanged looks. "Of course it doesn't, Het. Of course not. Now, how would you like some fresh coconut juice?"

"I can prove it!" I said. "I remember the day they first came through with the wires. We were up in the house when we heard a noise that sounded like chopping. My father and I came out to see what it was, and we saw workers trying to cut down one of our mango trees. That big one, right over there. My father asked them what they thought they were doing. The workers said that some of the mango tree's branches would be in the way of the wire, so they were cutting it down. My father said, well, why don't you just cut back the branches?

"The workers said that they never did that, they always cut down the whole trees. And they said there were other trees in the village they'd already cut down. I remember what the workers said about those trees. They said, 'They didn't put up much of a fight!' See? I even remember those words. 'They didn't put up much of a fight!'

"My father sent the workers away. He was as angry as I'd ever seen him. He went back inside to tell my mother. 'She'll be angry, too!' he was saying. But when he got inside, my mother was cutting some sour mango. She gave him a piece, and that calmed my father back down. I don't know if he ever did tell my mother about the chopping. He just ate the sour mango." I looked at my uncles triumphantly. "That proves it. If I can remember all that, I must have been there."

But Uncle Saam shook his head. "I don't know, Het. Your father could have told you that story himself."

Uncle Song agreed. "That's right," he said. "Sure, it started as an electricity story, but in the end it was all about sour mango!"

They chewed on sunflower seeds while I sat thinking.

"All right," I said. "What about this one? What about after the wires were already up? Remember? We had electricity then, but nobody could afford to buy any electrical equipment."

"I don't remember anything like that."

"No. That never happened around here."

"But it did! And then finally we got a light at the temple. Remember? Everybody crowded around just to watch it shine. You were there, too. I saw you! I stood right beside you! And the thing that we noticed was all the bugs that came flying around the light. More and more of them kept showing up from all over, and soon there was a big cloud. All the gnats from around our whole village were flying in to get close to that light. You even said that you recognized some of those bugs from out back of your house. By the second or third night, the cloud of bugs was so thick that we could hardly see the light anymore. It was just as dark as before we got the electricity!"

My uncles were giving me doubtful looks.

"It's hot," they were saying. "Are you sure you wouldn't like that coconut juice?"

"It's true!" I went on. "Don't you remember? Our village's bugs kept gathering there at the light. But the ones that suffered were the lizards. They couldn't figure out what happened to all the bugs they used to eat. Remember how skinny they got? We had all these skinny lizards going around looking hungry and confused. Then finally one lizard climbed up by the light, and that was it for the bugs. We all stood watching that first lizard having a feast up there. Soon there were more and more lizards up by the light, and the bugs were forced to go somewhere else. Why, you told me yourself that the reason it's so comfortable to sit around in our village after dark is because of what happened to all the bugs at that first temple light."

As I finished, my uncles were nodding slowly.

"You know, Het, you like to draw pictures. And we think that's great. We really do. But sometimes you have to remember. A picture is only a picture. Just because you draw something, that doesn't mean it really happened."

"That's right, Het. If you've been drawing pictures of temples lights and skinny lizards, that's OK by us. But you can't use your drawings to rewrite our history!"

Deep down I knew that my uncles were putting me on, that they remembered those events just as clearly as I did. But I knew they were testing me, too. They wanted to see if I was old enough to keep coming up with more stories, the way the adults in our village did, and I wanted to prove to them that I could.

So I was gritting my teeth and thinking my hardest. "Just a minute," I said. "I'll think of a new one. There were some more things about lights." Slowly another story came back to me. "I remember now. It was when we got the second light. That was at the headman's house, remember? And when he turned it on, the light at the temple got dimmer. It was only half as bright as it had been. And when we got the third light, at Khun Kru Chompoo's house, both of the first lights got dimmer, too." I stopped and looked at Uncle Song. "Why, you were the one who said that electricity was like a bucket of rice wine, because there's only so much to go around. I'm sure that was you."

Uncle Song was trying to remember. "I don't think I would have said something like that."

"Neither do I," said Uncle Saam. "That's much too clever for him. It's even too clever for me!"

"But there was another thing, too." Now I was sure that I had them. "This was after the grocer's husband bought the electric hair clippers. He set up that old barber's chair under the trees in front of the grocery, and he started giving us haircuts."

My uncles looked at me blankly.

"Don't you remember? Those clippers used so much electricity that the power kept going off whenever he used them. We were all going around with half our hair cut. And he used to race to get done before the power went out again. I know I was around for that, because look! I have half of a haircut right now!" And I pointed up to my head.

Uncle Song chuckled. "Het, we believe you about the hair clippers. But that's recent. Of course you were around for that."

"That's right," Uncle Saam said. "We had electricity for years before the hair clippers came along. You're talking about two different eras."

Uncle Song sighed and stood up. "The point is," he said, "if you ever hope to convince people of things, you'll need a better haircut than that. Come on. We'll take you down to the barber."

By the time we arrived, though, the electricity had already gone out. But that didn't matter. The barber said he knew where to find some especially fresh coconuts, and we followed him there.

EVEN THE HEAT HERE IS FRIENDLY

At last I was old enough go to a meeting at the headman's house.

I noticed everything that morning. I watched the headman most of all. Everyone went quiet when he talked; the puffs of smoke from his cigarette added emphasis. I noticed the grandparents, too. When they spoke, the rest of the villagers nodded in agreement at their wisdom, or laughed freely if the grandparent was making a joke.

"As you know," the headman began that morning, "for two years I've been requesting funds from the district for the things Slippery Stream Banks Village needs most urgently. A reservoir for rainwater. A pump and a pipeline up from the stream. A clinic. A doctor. Some new wells." He smoked for a while; he was an easygoing headman. "Today I'm privileged to tell you that the district has finally agreed to provide us some money."

People nodded and applauded; their clapping scattered cigarette ash and sunflower-seed shells around on the floor.

The headman held up his hand, which of course was holding his own cigarette.

"The problem," he said as he studied a small sheet of paper, "is that the money isn't for any of those things."

"What's it for?" asked someone. "We already have everything else."

"That's right. We put in the new toilets at school."

"Anyway. What else do we have any use for?"

"The money," the headman said, "is for an entrance sign in front of the village."

People scratched their heads.

"An entrance sign?" one of the grandfathers said. "What for?"

"To welcome visitors," said the headman. "And to let them know where they are."

"But no one ever comes here."

"Except us. And we know where we are already."

Nop's father spoke up. "What's the part about welcoming visitors? We can welcome everybody ourselves."

"And we always will," said the headman. "Now I'm not saying that an entrance sign is the best way to spend money in our village. But it's the district's money, and they want us to put up a sign. So that's what we're going to do."

The rest of the meeting was spent planning. Everyone had a suggestion for the new entrance sign. Some people preferred plain and basic. Others said it should show a map, or maybe the name of the abbot at the temple. A group led by my uncles wanted to think up a motto.

"I'll appoint two committees," the headman finally said. "One to think of a motto, the other to decide whether the sign should have a motto at all."

That night some of the villagers gathered at our house. They were full of ideas.

"It has to mention the stream. That's where we get our name, after all."

"But the stream is the name of the village. We don't have to put it on the sign twice," one of my aunts pointed out.

"How about HOME OF GRENADE HANDS? He's our most famous citizen."

"That's not bad. But a motto should tell what the place is like. It should talk about us."

"Well, what are we like?"

Everyone thought.

"It's hot here. That's something."

"How about EVEN THE HEAT HERE IS FRIENDLY? That wraps us up in a nutshell."

"That's good, but I've got another idea: GATEWAY TO SLIPPERY SWAMP. What do you think?"

"I like it, but remember, the swamp's all dried up!"

On and on they talked, trying out ideas. It became clear even to me that they did not want to come to a decision at all. They just wanted something to talk about until it was time to go home. They liked discussing much more than deciding.

At the next meeting, my uncles proposed our group's suggestions. The other committee listened politely, then said they had decided that the sign shouldn't have any motto.

"That way, our name will stand out on the sign," they said. "And it will save us from arguing over which motto is best."

People from both committees talked back and forth. Then the headman held up his hand.

"If you can't decide, it comes down to me. I propose that our sign just say WELCOME. Actually, that's the district's proposal; they sent it along with the funding. And since it's their money, WELCOME it is."

Uncle Song was shaking his head. "It's a missed opportunity," he said later. Yet he was the one who painted the word on the sign.

Everybody pitched in, of course. One of our village's traits was that even when we couldn't see the point of a thing, we did it as well as we could. Some people dug holes. Others worked with wood and cement. And the kids found plants to put in at the base of the sign. The day turned into a big celebration.

Before long the headman called another meeting. I felt like a regular now. This time the headman had an odd look on his face, and though he still held a cigarette, his free fingers were scratching his head.

"First of all, thank you for your work on the sign. It brings honor to all of us, since all of us helped. Today I have another announcement." As he went back to scratching his head, some ashes dropped into his hair.

"You'll remember that our sign was paid for by the district. We owe a great debt to them. But today," he began, then stopped. He unfolded a small piece of paper before continuing. "Most of you know that for years, we've been requesting money not only from the district, but also from the province, so that we can solve those same problems: the reservoir and the clinic and so on. Well, finally the province has come through."

People nodded. But this time they didn't applaud.

"There's a catch," someone said. "What's the catch?"

Another of our village traits: we learn fast.

"The catch," the headman said, "is that they want us to build an entrance sign."

Everybody began talking at once. Even Nop and I turned and talked to each other.

Only the headman stayed quiet. He waited and then held up his hand. "One thing you should know. This is the province, not the district. So this time the budget is bigger."

"We don't need bigger. We have one more sign than we need already."

"We should spend the budget on something we can use!"

The headman was shaking his head. "Let me explain how this works. We've been requesting money from the province for years. Now they give us enough to put up a sign. If we don't make the sign, they'll think we're ungrateful, and it will be years before they even think about helping us out again."

"But if we build a big sign with money from the province, the people from the district will feel slighted."

"We could put this one up somewhere else."

"Somewhere else? There's only one road."

"What about the side lane to Slippery Stream Bed Village?"

"We don't need an extra-big sign for them!"

"I'll appoint three committees," the headman decided. "Two to find the best place for the new sign, and the third to work out a compromise."

That night the same group of villagers came around to our house again. They were quieter this time.

"This is a tough one," they said.

"I used up all of my ideas on the motto."

"Why don't we make a long sign, lay it down, and use it as a road?"

"We could make a big sign and then turn it around. People would see it when they leave."

The discussion was warming up now.

"I say we make a big sign and put it up by the old one. Nobody has to know which is which. When the district people come, theirs is bigger. When the province is here, they win. What do you say?"

"We could make the new sign a little bit thicker. From the front, they'd look like they were the same size."

Finally Uncle Song turned to me. "Het, you've been sitting here listening all this time. Any ideas?"

As it turned out, I had been wondering what I'd recommend if I were on one of the committees, or even if I were the headman, and so I was prepared. "We could make a sign that says, 'Welcome to Slippery Stream Banks Village Clinic.' Then we'll be ready when the clinic gets built."

Uncle Song was staring at me. "Het, you're a genius. If we make a sign for the clinic, they'll have to build us one. It might work!"

At the next meeting, he volunteered my proposal. Heads were nodding all around the circle.

"We like that idea," a member of the other group said. "Now here's ours. We suggest putting the new sign out by the main road, ten kilometers away. We know people will still pass right by, as usual. But if we have a first-rate sign out there, at least they might wonder what they're missing."

There were more nods and sounds of approval. "This calls for a compromise," people were saying, and they turned to the compromise committee.

But the headman held up his hand. "With all due respect to the committees, our decision has been made for us already." He showed us a new sheet of paper. "I'd like to thank you for your first-rate suggestions. I think we can rest assured that the planning of Slippery Stream Banks Village will be in good hands for a long time to come. As it turns out, though, the province has handed down this order, and, as you all know, it's their money."

The headman read from the new sheet of paper. "'The generous funds provided to Slippery Stream Banks Village shall be used to construct a motto-free entrance sign just outside the village beside Township Road 102A, facing east.'"

We sat listening; then the stirring began.

"Why, that road no longer exists!"

"Nobody's used that road since the flood washed it out, years ago," said one of the grandfathers. "I was on the replacement committee myself!"

"That sign will be facing the ricefields. No one will see it but buffaloes and oxen."

"All of you are right," said the headman. "Obviously the province is going by maps that must be twenty years old. Maybe next year we can request that a new survey be done. But they'll never give us what we want next year if we don't follow their orders for this year. Now let's form committees to decide on the best day to put up the sign."

Uncle Song was shaking his head. "Another missed opportunity," I heard him say. Yet he became the head of the ground-breaking committee and helped dig holes for the new sign himself.

Again the day became a big celebration.

"This is fun," people were saying. "It's becoming a tradition."

"Where's the sign going in next month?"

"I've got a new motto: THE ENTRANCE-SIGN CAPITAL OF THAILAND."

We had to admit, the new sign was impressive. The province had sent out slabs of cement, with one letter of our village's name carved in each of the slabs. It was a long, low sign, and we had to walk way out into the ricefield before we could read the whole thing.

Then the headman called a new meeting. I was becoming so used to them that I sensed right away that something was different. Nop pointed out what it was.

"His cigarette," he said.

Sure enough, the headman was smoking a cigarette that was thicker and longer than the ones he had smoked at the earlier meetings, and it was putting out twice as much smoke. Once again, he was studying a sheet of paper.

"I don't know quite how to say this," he began. "As headman, I can lead this village only so far. Once we progress to the next level, my hands are tied. Then I follow the orders, not give them."

He took a long puff as he studied the paper.

"What's the bad news?" asked one of the grand-fathers.

"As you all know, for some time we've been humbly appealing to the national government for much-needed improvements, which I don't need to go into again. And, well, the government has finally responded."

No one nodded or applauded; a few people actually groaned.

"It's another entrance sign!"

"Even bigger this time!"

"Out in the middle of nowhere!"

Everyone chipped in an opinion. Then the head-man held up his oversize cigarette.

"The good news is that we don't have to build another entrance sign. The bad news"—he referred to the paper—"is that we've been...how did they say it? 'Redesignated.'"

"Redesignated?"

"What does that mean?"

"It means," the headman explained, "that we will no longer be a 'village.' Instead, we will become 'residential sector number two.'"

Everyone burst out talking as the headman sat smoking patiently. Finally one of the grandfathers raised his hand.

"May I ask when this redesignation takes place?"

The headman read over the sheet. "It doesn't say. Why?"

"Because," said the grandfather, and he cleared his throat, "I was born in Slippery Stream Banks Village, and I intend to die in Slippery Stream Banks Village, not in Slippery Stream Banks Residential Sector Number Two!"

All the adults shouted their agreement. So did some of the kids.

The headman was nodding. "I know how you feel. And I agree. But I should tell you that along with this redesignation, we'll be receiving more funds."

People changed their expressions. "More funds? For what?"

The headman consulted the sheet. "'The initial funding,'" he read, "'shall be used to make name changes on any existing entrance signs, as required.'"

I don't have to tell you that it was the outspoken grandfather himself who wound up painting the new name on our first entrance sign. But as for the second sign, that name was carved in cement, and it couldn't be changed quite so easily. The old name remained.

"Now it's even more useless," people said. "It faces the wrong way, and it gives the wrong name, besides!"

Then a strange thing happened. The night after the grandfather repainted the first entrance sign, we all went to sleep, as usual. But the next morning, a buzz went around through the village.

"The first entrance sign," people were saying. "It collapsed!"

Sure enough, the sign was in a heap on the ground. Everyone was talking at once.

"Who did it?"

"Something was wrong with the paint!"

"No, the paint was top quality. This is a curse!"

"A curse! The curse of the new village name!"

Of course, when the idea of a curse takes hold, no one lets go. Even the headman was convinced.

"I'll report this immediately," he said. "We're on solid ground here. If the new name is cursed, there's no way they can expect us to keep it."

"What about funding?" someone asked.

"New funds or not," said the headman, "we can't go on with a curse. Today it's this entrance sign. Who knows? Tomorrow it might be the school or the temple. And the day after that, the new entrance sign."

The same thought came to everyone at once. We ran through the village to the big useless sign.

The kids, who were the most used to running, arrived first. "It's still standing!" we shouted.

"It was protected by the old village name," said the adults when they caught their breath. "We've got to do all we can to take care of this sign—and to get our real name back!"

Some of us went over and swept dust off the sign. My uncles checked the foundation. And the headman went up to the sign carrying a coconut.

"This sign is the symbol of the good name of Slippery Stream Banks Village. It's up to all of us to keep this sign strong. On behalf of our village, I offer this coconut to the spirits who watch over our sign."

From that day on, it became our custom to place offerings at the base of the sign as a way to keep our village strong and to ward off new curses.

One morning as I was offering perfectly ripe mangoes up to the sign, a group of men stood nearby, talking.

"So who did it, anyway? I heard it was you. Did you tear down that old sign?"

"Not me. I can't find anybody who knows."

"Maybe it was a real curse, after all."

One of the grandfathers stood listening. He went over and patted the big cement sign.

"I've lived here a long time," he said to the group, "and I still can't tell a real curse from a fake one. But if there's one thing life in this village has taught me, it's that when you try to find a use for a thing you once thought was useless, it often turns out to be more useful than things that you used to have uses for." The grandfather let his words sink in. Then he went off to the temple.

The group of men stood there.

"Did you understand that?"

"Not really. Did you?"

"I'm not sure. But it sounded good, didn't it?"

"Yes, it did. You know, if we changed a few words here and there, and put in the name of the village, it might make a pretty good motto."

The men talked about that as they headed back through the field to the village.

RIPPO

Every boy in our village claimed to be the first one who had seen the poster go up at the grocer's. "I was buying fish sauce for my mother when the grocer unrolled it," one boy bragged.

"No, it was me!" said another. "The grocer asked me to hold up the corners while she taped it!"

Still another boasted that he had helped the deliveryman carry the poster in from the dusty supply truck.

With all those arguments going on, I knew it was useless to tell them what really did happen: that of course the first one who had seen it was me.

It's true. I was heading past just as the grocer turned away from taping the poster up to the wall. I couldn't help staring. Everything else in the grocery was dusty and sun-faded—the goods, the walls, and on hot days like that one, even the grocer herself. Our whole village was faded that way.

But the poster stood out. It was freshly unrolled and full of bright pictures. It was shiny. The grocer was proud of that poster. "That's the first piece of paper ever to make it all the way out to Slippery Stream Banks Village without losing its gloss," she said. She stopped a moment, startled. "Come to think of it, that's the first time I've ever used the word *gloss*."

I spent so much time looking at the colors and the shine of the poster that I almost forgot to read what it said. Rippo read the big letters across the top, and just below that was the word Contest.

That's about as far as I read before the grocery became crowded with the boys who would go around later claiming that they'd been there first.

Together, we read the details of the contest. It was run by Rippo, the Energy Drink, which we knew as one of the sponsors of Grenade Hands, our world-famous boxer. People had to send in labels from bottles of Rippo—ten labels for each chance—to be eligible to win one of the prizes shown on the poster.

Those prizes were what made us gape. Not the first prize, a pickup truck, or the two second prizes, motorcycles, or the five TV sets or ten rice cookers. We didn't care about them. Instead, we stared at the very bottom, at the last prize on the list: one hundred brand-new "tournament quality" soccer balls.

We had a soccer ball already, of course—the one that we used every day after school. That ball was scuffed and gray and flat. It made tired sounds when we kicked it. It was so old that no one could remember who it belonged to.

"Why, this scuff has been here since I was a boy," said Uncle Song one day when he stopped by our game.

But the ball on the poster was different.

"Look—it's black and white!" said one of the boys in the grocery.

"It's pumped up!"

"It's tournament quality!"

We stared at that poster so long that already it was losing its gloss.

We knew right away that we had to enter the contest. Our problem was that we were too young to drink Rippo. On top of that, we had no money to buy it.

"Everybody, talk to your parents at supper. Talk to your aunts and your uncles. Talk about nothing but Rippo!"

We agreed that we would.

"And another thing. Be on your best behavior. The better our manners are, the more Rippo our parents will buy."

"Be good, everybody."

"Be obedient!"

Everybody was. And, after supper, the group of villagers turned up at my house.

"What's all this about Rippo?" one of them said.

"How come my son volunteered to wash dishes?"

My father turned to me. I had told him and my mother about Rippo already. And I had washed the dishes at our house, too. "You'd better go upstairs, Het. This discussion may turn serious."

I went, of course. I wanted to be obedient. Besides, I could lie under my mosquito net and hear everything clearly. My father knew that. But the others didn't, and on some nights my father sent me upstairs so that the rest of the group would speak freely.

"The way I see this, either we're all in, or we're all out."

"I agree. This is a community project."

"Drinking Rippo? That should be an individual choice."

"It should be, but look. Suppose you drink it and I don't—and then we win the ball. I know my boy; he'll want to play with it just as much as yours."

"Good point. There might be resentment."

"I see what you mean. We have to stick together."

"Absolutely. Otherwise the kids will be divided."

"And maybe us, too. How will the ones who drink Rippo every day feel about the ones who shirk their community duties?"

"I say we all have to do our fair share for the sake of the village."

"I'm with you. But suppose we do win the ball. What will the kids want after that? Grass on the field?

A net for the goal? We ought to think about where all this could lead."

"You've got a point there. I was in the grocery today, and I saw how that poster clashes with the rest of the village. I'm not sure how much we want to get our kids thinking."

"I wondered about that, too. But I have faith in them. I'm sure the kids understand that this is a once-and-done deal. It begins and ends with the soccer ball."

"Besides, there's no guarantee that we'll win."

There were sounds of people nodding in agreement.

"So we're in?"

"All right, then. Everybody get ready to drink Rippo."

This time, I knew I was first. I ran into the rice-fields at sunup the next morning to let out a whoop.

I saw the other boys running out, too.

"Guess what?" they were shouting. "I was the first one to know!"

I'll always remember that next month; it is one of the most famous in our village's history. "The Rippo month," people call it, and there's no need to say more.

The other boys and I spent our free time down at the grocer's. When people came in to buy Rippo, we gave a big cheer, and we urged them to go ahead and drink two. We peeled off each label with care, and when we got ten, we placed them gently in an envelope with our village's name and address. It became a great honor to do the inserting.

"This could be the one," someone remarked about each entry, and we sealed the envelope solemnly.

And that month is when life in Slippery Stream Banks Village, where no one had ever used the word *hurry* before, speeded up.

We noticed it in little ways at first. Our parents spoke faster. Twitches became more pronounced. People were jumpy by the time they came in for their second or third bottles. We took to twisting the caps off for them and then leaving them in peace as they drank.

I saw changes in other things, too. Fathers who had always shuffled from place to place in our village were now darting. The rhythm of my own father's saw strokes, which hadn't changed since before I was born, grew quicker. And the villagers who came to our house at night never sat down anymore; now they paced. At first they bumped into one another a lot, but after a few nights each person had established a pattern. As people paced, they chewed sunflower seeds briskly.

It turned out that Rippo, the Energy Drink, really worked.

Odd jobs that had been neglected for years suddenly got tackled. Dead tree limbs were pulled down. Broken slats in our village's fences were replaced. Trash that had blown under bushes was picked up and disposed of. Dust built up on our hammocks.

It got to the point where no one could even appear to be resting. If someone happened to stretch out for just a few moments, someone else would rush off for a bottle of Rippo. "Pick up the slack!" you'd hear. "Don't forget your civic duty!" The embarrassed offender would gulp down the Rippo and come back to life.

"What would happen if you sprinkled Rippo on a rice plant?" someone wondered.

"Can buffaloes drink that?"

"I drank a bottle, and now I can't keep up with myself," said one of the grandfathers.

Our village had caught "Rippo fever," as Nop's father called it. We were still as friendly and cheerful as ever, only now we were cheerful at a much quicker pace. In the middle of it all was the grocer, who found herself ordering more and more Rippo—and more envelopes, too.

At last the month ended, and the day of the big drawing came. None of us boys slept at all that night; we didn't need Rippo to stay wide awake. It was decided that the headman, Uncle Song, and two other men would go into town for a newspaper so that the village could learn the contest results right away.

We waited down at the grocer's.

We tried sitting and talking about the dogs trotting by, but soon we were up pacing, too.

"What if we win?" we were asking. "Who gets to take the first kick?"

"Who gets to keep the ball the first night?"

"No one. The first night, we sleep in a circle at the temple, with the ball right in the middle."

We paced some more.

"Do you think we'll be famous?"

"There's no doubt. Villages all over the country want to win soccer balls."

"That's right. Our picture will be in all the newspapers."

"Suppose we don't win a soccer ball. Suppose we win the pickup truck instead."

"No. Don't say that. Don't even think about that."

"Maybe we could trade in the pickup for a soccer ball."

"No. They have rules against that. I think they're on the back of the poster."

"If we win the pickup, the headman will keep it. That's how that works."

"Listen, everybody. We've got to stop thinking about pickups. Remember. We entered this contest to win a soccer ball, and we won't be satisfied with anything less."

All this time, the grocer had been sitting nearby, listening. Now she finally spoke. "It's none of my business, but aren't you boys getting your hopes up awfully high?"

"We're just preparing ourselves," we told her.

"You can do as you please, of course. But don't you ever listen when you go to the temple? Getting your hopes up is a standing invitation to letdown."

"Oh, we listen, all right," we said. She was the grocer, and she often gave us sunflower seeds free. We liked her. But she obviously had no idea how it felt to look forward to winning a new soccer ball. We went right back to talking about winning.

Actually, we had another reason to ignore her. We had never known what it was like to want something we didn't already have. When we wanted mangoes, we climbed a tree and picked them. If we wanted adventure, we hiked to the next bend in the stream. But wanting a new soccer ball? That gave us hope, which for us was a new kind of feeling.

In the evening we got ready to welcome the men back from town. By now it was not just our group of boys; the whole village had come down to the grocer's to await the good news. Some people wondered how we would manage to go back to our old, normal lives after the drawing.

"But our lives won't be normal," we reminded them. "Remember, we'll have a new ball."

At last the men came back down our lane. They had taken the bus from town, then ridden a motorized cart out to our village. Now they were walking right up to the crowd at the grocer's, smiling widely.

"We won!" shouted the boys.

"Not so fast," said the headman. "We haven't checked yet. We wanted to share the excitement with you." He held up the newspaper. In the corner was a headline: RIPPO CONTEST WINNERS ANNOUNCED: SEE PAGE 8.

The crowd stirred as the headman opened to page 8 and then immediately covered it with another section of the paper.

"We can slide this down line-by-line so that we'll be just as excited as you are," he explained.

He cleared his throat, gave a smile, and then slid down the paper.

"First prize of a new pickup truck goes to Mr. Sangkhom Jaitip of Bangkok," he read.

We cheered.

"All right! We didn't win the pickup!"

Our hopes mounted.

The headman passed the newspaper to Uncle Song; the four men took turns reading names. We cheered again when we didn't win the motorcycles or televisions, and we sighed with relief when our name didn't appear under "rice cookers."

"The hardest part's over," we said.

"Everything's working out perfectly!"

The headman read the next line very slowly. "One hundred last prizes of brand-new tournament quality soccer balls go to the following."

"That's us!" we shouted.

"Here it comes!"

The first winner was a boy from a place that we'd never heard of.

"Good for him," we said.

"He's one of us!"

"We'll start a club for the winners!"

The second name wasn't ours either.

"That's all right. Two has never been our lucky number."

"Still ninety-eight more names to go."

I guess it was around number thirty or forty that people's reactions changed. Hearty congratulations to the winners gave way to an odd, nervous laughter.

On and on the men read. There were stray comments from the crowd. "I've been there," a man said as one hometown was read. "Oh, that's a nice name," said one of the mothers. But mostly we stood quiet and still.

Uncle Song read the ninety-ninth winner, then handed the paper back to the headman.

"One more to go," he said grimly. "Remember. In a contest like this, being one hundredth is just as good as being the first." He took a deep breath, then looked at the last name on the list.

The headman's eyes popped open, and he brought the paper right up to his face. For a moment we thought we had won. But when the headman looked up again, his mouth was hanging wide open.

"Number one hundred," he said, speaking so slowly that no one would have guessed he'd spent the last month drinking more bottles of Rippo than anyone else in the village, "Number one hundred is a community entry from"—he swallowed very hard—"from Slippery Stream Bed Village, Slippery Stream District, Three Streams Province."

Everyone was talking at once. "That's us," people were saying. "Isn't it?"

"Did he say Stream Banks or Stream Bed?"

"Read that again."

The headman rechecked the newspaper, and he showed it to the rest of the men.

"Number one hundred is Slippery Stream Bed Village. Not Slippery Stream Banks. It says Slippery Stream Bed." He shook his head. "I'm sorry."

For a moment we stood there, confused. We hadn't won. How could it possibly have happened? While we were waiting for that to sink in, we heard a big shout. We turned and looked off across the ricefields toward Slippery Stream Bed Village. Big whoops of joy were rising up over there, carrying back across the ricefields to us.

"It's all right," the headman was trying to say. "You win some, you lose some. Buck up, everybody. You can't keep a good village down." A few adults nodded, out of respect for the headman. But our group of boys had been so sure of winning that suddenly we felt as if the soccer ball had been stolen right from us.

I can't account for what everyone else did after the drawing. I know I wound up staggering down the lane, with no idea where I was headed. Some boys were still staring toward Slippery Stream Bed Village, and I saw others slumped against the trunks of coconut trees, stunned.

Then something came to me, and I staggered back to the grocer's.

"Sorry to bother you again," I managed to say. "I know we didn't win, but would you mind if I took one last look at the poster?"

Another boy staggered in. And another boy came in after that. Soon the grocery was filled up with boys, just as it had been that first day.

"I'm sorry about your new soccer ball, boys," said the grocer. "The least I can do is offer you sunflower seeds."

We thanked her, but we were in no mood to chew. It was a long time before any of us even spoke.

"What happened?" someone finally asked.

"Maybe we didn't send in enough entries."

"Are you sure we followed the rules? That poster has a lot of fine print."

"That's not what it was. We should have asked for a blessing at the temple. I bet that's where we went wrong."

"You're right. We should have taken the entries down to the abbot."

"Maybe we deserved not to win."

We were still talking about that when the headman stepped in with an odd look on his face.

"Uh, sorry to bother you boys at a time like this," he said. "I just got word on what happened over at Slippery Stream Bed Village." The headman stopped for a moment and cleared his throat. "Apparently, they weren't going to enter at all. Their grocer never even bothered to unroll the poster. Then on the very last day someone noticed it. They found some Rippo bottles in the garbage, ripped off the labels, and jammed them in an old envelope. That was their village's entry. It was almost like an afterthought." He shook his head helplessly. "I'm sorry, boys. I thought you might like to know." The headman went out.

We stood there a long time again.

"An afterthought," someone said.

"They sent in one entry."

"From the garbage!"

"And now they've got our new ball."

We let that sink in.

"They're probably down at their temple right now, getting ready to sleep in a circle."

"Or measuring their goals for new nets."

"Or planning to come show off their soccer ball to us."

The oldest boy stepped forward. "Well, they can't show it to me. I couldn't care less about soccer. I quit!" And he reached out for a sunflower seed.

"Me, too. Who needs it?"

"I'm taking up boxing!"

"From now on, it's badminton for me!"

Soon we were all chewing sunflower seeds. By the time we left the grocery, we felt much better.

"I bet no one in our village ever plays soccer again!"

"Or enters a contest!"

"Or buys Rippo, the Energy Drink!"

We were laughing and agreeing and spitting out sunflower-seed shells as we made our way home down the lane.

Of course, things didn't turn out exactly the way we predicted. Well, the grocer no longer stocked Rippo; it turned out that our village got all the energy it needed from coconut juice. But before long, men quietly dusted off their hammocks and lay down. Other men stretched out nearby. Dead limbs appeared in the trees, and trash that blew under bushes just stayed there. And by the end of that very same week, our group of boys was back on the soccer field after school, not only kicking that old, scuffed-up ball, but liking it.

Almost as if nothing had changed.

GRILLED BANANAS

By the time we finished ninth grade, which was as high as our school went up to, most of my friends were ready to go off to find work in Bangkok.

Nop and I were two of the luckier ones. He planned to stay and help his family farm its way through the drought. I was going to help my father make tables. He didn't really have enough for two people to do, but it kept the work in the family. More important than that, it was a way for me to stay home.

Then, on one of my last days at school, Khun Kru Surasak came up beside me.

"Let's talk," he said.

We sat under the jackfruit tree in back of the building, the same place where Grenade Hands got started. People said that if you checked the soil there carefully, you could still find fibers from the rice sacks that he had punched loose from their ropes, long ago.

Khun Kru Surasak didn't have a rice sack; he had a letter. "I never told you about this," he said as we sat in the shade, "but I sent some of your drawings to an art school in the city. And, to make a long story short, they liked them." He showed me the letter. "You have a chance for a scholarship, Het."

Right away I refused—politely, of course, which is the way of our village. "I appreciate that, Khun Kru Surasak. But I have work to do here. I'm going to be my father's assistant."

"I know about your plans, Het. But I've seen the look on your face when you get a fresh sheet of paper. I can tell you love drawing. This is a chance to make it your life. A scholarship like this would be an honor."

"I'm sorry, Khun Kru. But the city is too far away."

"It's not far away if you live there." Khun Kru Surasak smiled. "Let me tell you about the Three Streams School of Art. It's a real high school, but they emphasize artwork. They have top-quality paintbrushes and paper. They have desks without gouges. And if you go there, you can stay at my family's house. We have an extra room, Het."

I knew that Khun Kru Surasak wanted to help me, so I took my time answering. "It sounds perfect," I said. "But I can't go away from my family. My sister would have to bring water back from the well by herself." The thought of it made me shake my head no.

"You can always come back here later. Art school won't last forever."

I thought of something else. "What about Nop?"

Khun Kru Surasak hesitated. "Between you and me, Het, you're the one the school wants. It's very competitive. That's why it would be such an honor."

He asked me to think it over. All I had to do was submit a new set of drawings to the Three Streams School of Art by the end of the month.

"Find things to draw," he advised me. "Make it your very best work."

On my way home I climbed the staircase that led up to nothing. It was a good place for me to get thinking done. Up there, I saw things from a different angle.

The top step was where those messages had appeared over the years. The latest one said,

Be careful—the next step is

and then a line of paint trailed to the edge, as if the writer had fallen off the staircase before the message was finished. It was kind of a joke, I guess, and we still didn't know who had written it. From time to time, various teenagers had come under suspicion. But they left the village to find work, and those messages went right on appearing. Some people suspected Uncle Song. It was his staircase, after all, and this was certainly his kind of joke. But he had never mentioned anything about it, and that wasn't his style. When he had a joke going, he couldn't hold it inside. He kept making hints and poking fun until the joke gave him some kind of payoff. To him, the payoff was what made a joke worthwhile, and he had never said a word about the messages.

So they were still a mystery. By now, though, no one even tried to find out who wrote them. In a way, we didn't want to know, because we had gotten used to having that mystery around, and if we solved it, we had no idea what might come along in its place.

I sat on the top step that day, thinking of my two choices in life: stay in the village, work with my father, and try to become headman—or go off to become a world-famous artist.

When I thought about becoming the headman, it seemed like a never-ending struggle. I would have to attend meetings and work hard. I had to earn everyone's trust. One slip, it seemed, and the whole village would know, and someone else would move ahead of me on the list. Becoming the headman would prove that I had lived the right way all my life, and that now I was ready to live the right way on behalf of my village.

Becoming a world-famous artist was different. It seemed much easier. It seemed that all I had to do was decide, "OK, I will be a world-famous artist," and just like that, it would happen. As I sat on the staircase, I boiled it down to two steps. First, going off to study at the Three Streams School of Art; second, becoming world-famous. That's all it would take. Compared to the lifelong challenge of striving to be headman, becoming a world-famous artist felt like the easy way out.

I was still on the staircase when two of my friends sprinted past.

"Grilled bananas, Het!" they called out, then kept running.

I followed the scent down the lane and found that my aunts were in charge of the grilling. Already a crowd had gathered. People had settled in and were happily munching away. That wasn't surprising. Our philosophy was that if someone was going to make food, the least we could do was spend the rest of the day eating.

The bananas that day were especially good.

"Perfect," someone said. "One day later, and they would have been overripe."

My grandmother agreed. "These are the best we've had since the day those cats got into a fight by the grill. Remember?"

Everyone remembered. But nobody could agree just how many years ago that had been—or how many cats had been in the fight.

Not far from the grill sat Khun Kru Chompoo. She had retired by then, so she no longer wore her uniform or gave famous quizzes. But we all still considered her our teacher.

I went over and greeted her politely.

Khun Kru Chompoo was peeling bananas, getting them ready for my aunts. It turned out that she was one of the fastest banana peelers in our village.

"Oh, there you are, Het," she said. "I've been looking for you."

"You have?" I said, as she peeled yet another banana.

"Khun Kru Surasak showed me your drawings," she said. "I'm sure you'll keep up the good work."

I couldn't get used to the idea that anyone besides Khun Kru Surasak was interested in what I was drawing. "Uh, thank you, Khun Kru. Thank you very much."

Just then Uncle Song spoke up.

"This gives me an idea for a business," he said. "Why don't we sell grilled bananas in the city? They've got nothing nearly this good, believe me. We could support the whole village with these. What do you say? Who's in?"

He was still coming up with details when my mother came over to me. "Run home and bring more bananas," she said. "We're almost out."

Behind our house, I found two branches full of bananas. I was carrying them back when it happened.

I looked over and saw the whole group sitting there under a mango tree, eating bananas. My aunts were grilling and laughing away. But everyone found a way to help out. Some people mixed the sweet coconut sauce we dipped the bananas into. Others tore off pieces of banana-tree leaves that we used in place of saucers or trays. Children were serving their grandparents. Dogs nosed in from the sides, hoping to get their fair share.

"That's it," I realized. "That is the picture I'll draw."

I stood there taking it in. The youngest girl in the village tilting her head up toward her mother for the next bite. My own mother, who had a gift when it came to the coconut sauce, giving pointers to my little sister. My father dragging in a new sack of charcoal. Smoke on its way up from the grill.

"Yes," I was thinking. "I could draw that."

Maybe it was that day's bananas, or it might have been that batch of coconut sauce, but after I got back to the group, suddenly pictures jumped at me from all sides.

Uncle Song was still outlining his latest idea. "We'll call them Slippery Stream Banks Village Grilled Banana Snacks," he was saying. "What do you think about that?"

"Has a ring to it, Song," someone said, and my uncle beamed with anticipation.

"Now, there is a picture," I said to myself.

A woman who had been taking a nap came down the lane, giving an embarrassed laugh and holding out a fresh bunch of bananas to make up for coming so late.

"There is another," I said.

A boy, caught off guard by an extra-hot banana, juggled it until it cooled down.

"I could draw all of these things," I was thinking.

While everyone was still laughing about the boy's juggling, which was bound to become as famous as the catfight, I got up to go home and start working.

"Look at that," someone said. "I never saw Het walk away from grilled bananas before."

Everyone forgot the juggling for a moment and turned toward me.

"He probably wants to get a head start making tables. Hey, Het! The tables can wait! The bananas are ready right now!"

"Eat your fill now, Het, or later on you'll be sorry. You don't want to miss out."

"We need your appetite here!"

I smiled and stood where I was.

But even my aunt called out. "You can't leave now, Het. I've got three bananas here to the side, just the way you like them. I was grilling them especially for you!"

I knew my village; I had no choice. I sat back down. Immediately my aunt sent the perfectly grilled bananas over to me. "Plenty more where those came from," she said. Then she was grilling some more, especially for somebody else.

In no time at all, I had finished the first grilled banana.

Uncle Song sat watching. "Did you see that?" he asked my parents. "Keep feeding him grilled bananas, and you'll never get him away from under this tree!"

He laughed at that, and my parents did, too. I guess I laughed along. Soon others joined in. As we ate those bananas that day, our laughter built slowly, and it lasted. It rose through the branches, spread down the lane, and then, like the dust, settled down over our village.

ABOUT THE AUTHOR

Tom Glass taught in the provinces of Udon Thani and Mahasarakham, both in northeastern Thailand, for sixteen years. His previous work of fiction, also set in Thailand, is *Even a Little Is Something: Stories of Nong*. He lives near Washington, DC, with his wife, Noke, and their son, Nat.

www.ingramcontent.com/pod-product-compliance
Lightning Source LLC
Chambersburg PA
CBHW032009170626
46807CB00006B/2724